ARCADE MANNA

Arcade Manna

This is a work of fiction. Names, characters, places, and incidents either are the product of the author's imagination or are used fictitiously. Any resemblance to actual persons, living or dead, events, or locales is entirely coincidental

Copyright © 2022 Tyler H. Jolley

Cover Art and Design by John Hackett

Interior by Melissa Williams Design

All rights reserved.

Published in the United States by Tyler H. Jolley

ISBN: 978-1-7373296-5-7 (print)
    978-1-7373296-8-8 (eBook)

ARCADE MANNA

TYLER H. JOLLEY

JACK NEAL BOOTH

*I dedicate this to 7-Eleven
on 25 100 West and Maeser Highway
where we played all our arcade games growing up.*

001:

Bastian ignored the blistering heat beating through the Arcade's windows. He craned his neck, searching for a better view of Milt. The eighty-five-year-old man sat in front of *Water Bliss,* leaning close to the monitor, his bony fingers perched above an array of colored buttons on the control panel. His fingers, covered by elbow-length, rust-colored gloves, had long ago lost their rapid fluidity. Now, his hands shook slightly, and he struggled to tap the buttons as quickly as he once did.

Bastian's view of the Arcade console was blocked. He spotted an opening and slipped between the two adults before him, sidling up next to Milt. On the monitor, a young boy whom Milt controlled carried an empty bucket. He stood at the edge of a tree line across from a raging river. Separating the two was a vast expanse of land dotted with tigers.

"Hey, Bastian," Milt said, his eyes glued to the screen. "How ya doin'?"

"Been camping here for a while. Was hoping to make it out on the west side but couldn't risk another life."

Bastian glanced at the top left of the monitor. A single heart flashed. Milt had already lost two lives. One more, and he would have to restart from the beginning, something nobody had time for today.

"You got it. The worst that can happen is we go without water for tonight."

Milt ignored him, blinking the sweat away from his eyes. He wore a tight-fitted rubber cap on his head. Small yellow lightbulbs surrounded the brim, and wires extended out the top, connecting to an unseen panel on top of the cabinet.

From the speaker grill, the artificial roar of a tiger rose over the sound of the rushing river. Milt took a deep breath, then pressed his fingers into two buttons. His character ran forward. Milt pressed another button when he approached the first tiger, and the character moved to the right, avoiding the beast.

The breath of the other spectators was warm against the back of Bastian's neck. He refrained from expressing his annoyance. Typically, the Arcade was never this full, but this was Milt's concluding game, the last time he would ever collect water for the town 55178, his final moments before the Lives Out Ceremony.

"You nervous?" Bastian asked. He leaned in close to Milt.

"No. I'm ready to go." Milt dodged a few more tigers, winking at Bastian as he drew nearer to the river. On the top left of the monitor, Milt's XP flashed: 85/100. He'd been stuck at that number for two years. Most players eventually reached experience Level 100 and Leveled Up, but some didn't. Milt was one of the few.

A bead of sweat trickled down Milt's forehead, and Bastian wiped it away for him.

"Thanks," Milt said just as he pressed two more buttons and his character reached the river, unscathed by the tigers. "Now for the water." He pressed another button off to the side, and his inventory screen popped up, revealing one lonesome brown bucket. He selected that, returned to the playing screen, and waited as his character used the bucket to scoop water from the river.

When the character was finished, his bucket now sloshing with water, Milt returned the item to his inventory. The Arcade erupted with applause. Milt pressed a button indicating forward movement, and his character fell into the river and floated away. The words "GAME OVER" flashed on the monitor before the lights on Milt's rubber cap went dim, and he leaned back in his chair, breathing a sigh of relief.

The spectators swarmed Milt, clapping him on the shoulders, greeting him over the sound of applause and excited chatter. Bastian ignored all of them, trying his best not to let the situation get him down. He knew there was honor in a Lives Out Ceremony, but he still hated them. After today he would never see Milt again. The Spawning would choose someone new to play *Water Bliss* once Milt's vitals flatlined, and Bastian would be left with one less friend.

After a few minutes of celebration, Milt took the cap off his head, revealing tufts of gray, wispy hair, and removed his gloves. He motioned to Bastian, who broke from his stupor of thought and helped the old man to his feet. "Time to go," he said, leaning on Bastian as he hobbled out of the Arcade.

When they exited through the doors, the glaring sun momentarily blinded Bastian. He held his free arm over his eyes, keeping a tight grip on Milt, so neither of them stumbled.

Lining the steps leading to the Arcade were dozens of

townsfolk. Bastian recognized some of them—mostly the professional gamers—and was relieved so many people had turned up to celebrate Milt's last day.

Once they descended the steps, they turned left, finding another giant huddle of people. While most of them were courteous enough to turn and wave to Milt, some were not, their focus solely dedicated to the five rusted steel bins mounted to the side of the Arcade building. Next to the Five Bins was a three-thousand-gallon cistern for water with a copper spout protruding from the bottom. It was wrapped with cloth and brown string, a feeble attempt to fix a leak.

Bastian chuckled when he spotted a group of children standing close to the Five Bins, heads bowed in whispers, occasionally glancing up to look at the brown stains across the lip of the bins. No doubt they were discussing the rumors surrounding the Five Bins, the same rumors Bastian had heard when he was younger. Legend had it, the stains on the bins came from human blood. Apparently, many had tried breaking into the bins before they automatically opened, but the lids had clamped down on their hands, cutting them clean off. One guy had even tried climbing inside the bin, but the automatic lids had closed on him and cut him in half. As a kid, Bastian had believed the rumors fully, which was probably why he'd never tried breaking into the bins, but he wasn't sure he believed them now.

A collective sigh escaped the group surrounding the water cistern when only half of the tank filled for the day.

"That's all," one woman said, tossing her hands in the air.

"I'm so sorry," Milt said. "It used to be three thousand gallons a day." This drew Bastian's attention. "But my old age has made me slow, lazy. The town needs more than fifteen hundred gallons a day, Bastian."

"I know, Milt," he said.

Up ahead, the townsfolk had gathered around the Lives Out Monument. It was a dark stone slab laid flat on top of four concrete blocks. The names of those who had been killed by the town, sacrificed by the people, were etched into its surface in small lettering.

Soon, someone would add Milt's name to the list.

Bastian swallowed the lump in his throat, ignoring the cheers of bystanders, as he led Milt slowly toward the stone slab.

002:

Milt opened his mouth to say something, but Callum interrupted them. He emerged from the crowd, offering his forearm to Milt for balance. Callum was shorter than Bastian by twelve inches. While he was naturally more muscular than Bastian, he was still skinny, his clothes hanging awkwardly off his shoulders. His red hair was shaggy and a brighter shade than Bastian's buzzed, burnt orange.

"How's the old man?" Callum asked, offering Milt a smile.

Milt grinned at him half-heartedly and nodded at the stone slab ahead of them. "I'm about to die, so about as good as a man can be."

"Sorry to ask," Callum said, frowning. "Just not sure what to say."

"You two have your whole lives to say things. Don't fret about right now."

They walked the rest of the way to the Lives Out monument in silence, Milt hanging onto their wrists for support. The blaring sun bounced off the concrete walls.

It was a scalding day. Bastian had only been outside for a few minutes, and he was already sweating. The pits of his brown shirt were darkening.

As they approached the stone slab, the circle of people broke apart to allow Milt through. Dr. Soren stood next to the slab, a syringe in her gloved hand. Her bushy red hair was tied into a bun, and she wore a white lab coat.

"Milt," she said, bowing her head to him.

"Dr. Soren," he said. He let go of Bastian and Callum and climbed onto the stone slab. Bastian winced when the old man's knees scraped the edge of the platform. Around them, the crowd murmured and whispered.

Bastian caught sight of Odette, who stood on the other side of the monument. She wiped a tear from her freckled face. He fought the sudden urge to go to her. *She doesn't need to be comforted,* he thought to himself. *We've all seen this before.*

Dr. Soren raised her hand, and the crowd fell silent. Almost the entire town was here today, sweltering beneath the sun. Bastian's eyes wandered to the concrete walls that reached so high, he could barely see the top. Their drabness was ubiquitous and depressing. Deep down, Bastian felt some relief for Milt. The old man was finally escaping these impenetrable walls, going somewhere far beyond them.

"Attention!" Dr. Soren said. She spun in a slow circle as she spoke, addressing the whole crowd at once. "Today, we sacrifice Milt. For the last forty years, he has played *Water Bliss.* Every single day for the last forty years! Milt has devoted his energy and his time to ensure we had clean water. Many claim my job is the most important, that Simon's job is the most important, but I'm here to tell you that you're wrong. Without water, we have no chance of survival. More than three days without water, and we would be in a bad way."

She reached down and patted Milt, who grabbed her hand. His eyes glimmered with tears.

"Thank you, Milt, for your service. You will never be forgotten."

The crowd surrounding him all said, "Thank you," in unison.

She lowered the syringe to the crook of Milt's left arm and poked it into his vein. "It'll only be a minute," she said. Then she pressed down on the syringe. The clear liquid inside disappeared, funneling into Milt's arm.

With his free hand, Milt waved Bastian and Callum forward. Callum, who was fighting his hardest not to cry, almost broke at this gesture. Here Milt was—one of the oldest residents of 55178—using his last remaining moments to speak to him.

Callum pulled Bastian forward, and they both fell to their knees next to Dr. Soren, who had withdrawn the syringe and stepped away quietly.

"Listen, you two," Milt said, tilting his head toward them. His lips were blubbering, shining with spit, his eyes already misting over. "This life is cruel, monotonous, and hopeless in a way." He coughed, not bothering to cover his mouth with his arm. His fingertips were shaking, and his eyelids acted heavy, threatening to droop closed. "The best happiness you can find is in friendship. Be kind to others, serve them, love them. That's how you'll be happy."

The crowd leaned forward, trying to catch a glimpse of Milt's final words. He ignored them. "I hope one of you is chosen to play *Water Bliss*. I think—" He paused, struggling with his breath. "I think that would be lovely."

Then Milt closed his eyes. One last breath escaped

his chest. The town remained still for a moment, silently honoring Milt's life. Bastian let loose a few tears. He'd seen this nearly a dozen times before. Ever since he'd arrived in 55178, the town had sacrificed a gamer once every year or two. Milt was just another name in a long line of them. But this time had been different for Bastian. He'd been close to Milt, friends with him, and now Milt was gone. *Was it really worth having friends? The death of a gamer always hurt.*

A few minutes later, the crowd dispersed. Bastian took hold of Milt's hand one last time, and then Callum pulled him away. It was time to go to work. The town wasn't going to feed itself.

003:

For the first time in many months, Bastian found it hard to concentrate at work. Stocking shelves wasn't a difficult task by any means, and he knew that, but he was distracted. Milt's death had done something to him, made him feel a strange way. He hadn't identified what the feeling was yet, but he was working on it.

"Hey, you good?" Callum asked. He stood down the aisle, reaching as high as he could to deposit a tin package labeled "OAT CEREAL" on the top shelf.

"Just distracted," Bastian said, removing a package of food from the pallet next to him and placing it on a random shelf.

The grocery store was one of the larger buildings in 55178. It was lined with rows and rows of shelves, all of them stocked with food that would only last twenty-four hours. Simon, their boss and the one who played *Blissful Grocer* to collect food for the town, always ordered just enough food so it wouldn't spoil the by the next day. Everything rotting by the next day was a phenomenon that everyone in 55178 accepted as normal. Everyone understood that none of the food would last more than one day, but Simon always played the game extra to try to get as much food as he could.

Bastian's eyes settled on the tin packaging in his hand. Bold, black lettering identified the food within as "FLOUR." He wondered, not for the first time, who packaged the food for 55178. Who wrote labels on the packaging to make it easier for them to sort? Who had built the giant concrete walls and the Arcade? Who designed the system by which they lived?

Many people enjoyed discussing these unanswerable questions, but nobody had ever provided a probable solution. It was just how the world worked, they'd say. You played the games, collected what you needed, and it would appear in the Five Bins outside the Arcade.

"Do you think sacrificing somebody is necessary?" Bastian asked, dropping his hands to his side and facing Callum.

"What do you mean?" he asked, preoccupied with his task.

"I mean, we view death as something sad. We're constantly discussing suicide, being taught about how it's never the right thing to do. Yet, when we murder someone and call it 'sacrifice,' it's treated as a good thing."

Callum shrugged. "It *is* a good thing, though."

Bastian rolled his eyes. Callum didn't understand. He never really had. So many people in 55178 never questioned anything beyond their day-to-day activities. They were happy doling out the same task regularly. Even most pro gamers were content with slowly building their XP, doing the same thing day after day after day, never wondering what was beyond the giant concrete walls surrounding the town. Bastian almost envied people like

Callum. He wished he could ignore the primal urges within him to understand the world better.

All of this made him think of Milt. Only a few hours had passed since the old man's sacrifice. His body was probably still on the stone slab. Only later would a man named Garvy take it to a far corner of the town and burn it to ash. He didn't envy Milt for his death, but rather for a new beginning. Nobody knew what happened to somebody after they died. Most people refused to even discuss it. But Bastian knew there had to be something.

The people Bastian truly envied were allowed to enter the Elevator and descend to unknown depths. Few people ever got the opportunity; the Elevator only opened for the pro gamers who reached 100 XP. Bastian had known a few pros who reached 100 XP and got into the Elevator. Within twenty-four hours, their vitals flatlined, and they were never heard from again. Whether they died or lived, nobody knew. For Bastian, that was where genuine excitement began—a journey into the unknown.

"I do miss him," Callum said.

Bastian shook his head, realizing he'd been sitting still, doing nothing for quite some time. He returned to stocking the shelves, reaching deep into the bin and pulling out whatever he found.

"He was a good guy," Bastian said, agreeing with Callum.

"Maybe sacrifice is wrong," Callum admitted as he neatly stacked some tins of rice. "But what else is there to do? Milt was only collecting half a tank of water per day. The town needed more than that. Nobody else can hook up to the Arcade games unless the player's vitals flatline." Callum rubbed at a spot just below his right wrist. Bastian absentmindedly copied his movements.

Everybody in 55178 had the same small, hard lump

in their wrists, in the same exact spot. It was a tiny microchip that served only one function: to monitor a person's vital signs. It was impossible to remove unless one decided to cut off their hand. Fused to the muscle, the microchip was as much a part of people as their tongues and eyes.

Bastian thought of Thayer, the technician who resided in the back of the Arcade. He was the only one who had access to the computer that monitored everyone's vital signs. While he kept an eye on as many people as possible, he mainly focused on the gamers. Their vitals were literally vital to the survival of 55178.

"I don't know," Bastian said, answering Callum's question. His gut still felt hollow from watching Milt get sacrificed, and his mind was distracted with a dozen different thoughts. He was tired of working. He wanted to go home and lie down.

He reached into the bin again and pulled out a tin box, this one labeled "SUGAR CEREAL." When he lifted it to the shelf, something *clinked* inside the box. He opened the cereal box without a second thought, pulled out the foil packaging containing the food, and poured out the empty box. A small, torn piece of paper attached to a paper clip fell into his open palm. He flipped it over. It was a part of a drawing. He couldn't make sense of it, though he was sure it fit somewhere in Simon's notebook.

"Found one," Bastian said, lifting it so Callum could see.

"Well," Callum said, slightly disappointed, "there goes my evening."

004:

That night, Bastian and Callum crowded into Simon's office at the back of the grocery store. It was a poorly lit room, barely big enough for any guests, but this was the only place Simon felt comfortable discussing his conspiracy theories. The only ventilation came from a small window that Simon never opened above the desk, so the room always smelled musty.

"All right, the last of the food is gone, and I've closed the store." Simon paused when he entered his office, taking a moment to stare at Bastian and Callum. Simon was only two years older than them, but he seemed much older than twenty. He was a tall man whose hair was constantly parted to the left. He wore a black hoodie at all times—how he survived in the unending heat of 55178 was beyond Bastian. "You guys okay?" he asked.

"Sure," Callum said, "why?"

"Milt," Simon said. He didn't elaborate further.

"We're okay," Bastian said, even though it wasn't particularly true. "Here you are." He extended the piece of paper he'd found in the cereal box earlier. Simon took it from him, handling it delicately, as if it were threatening to crumble to dust in his hands.

"There aren't very many pieces left," he said, setting the paper down on his desk and reaching into the lowest drawer for a bulging envelope. He cleared the desk and began laying pages from the envelope out.

As he did this, the office door opened, and Odette stepped through. She was a bright spot in the drab room. Her long, bright red hair framed her sharp cheekbones and crystal-blue eyes. A baggy yellow shirt hung off her slender shoulders. While she wore jeans like the rest of them, she'd patched holes in them with fabric from other clothing. Her belt was made from the fabric of old shirts. She was the most eccentric of Bastian's friends, and her happy attitude only added to that.

"You started without me?" she asked, feigning offense.

Bastian didn't understand why, but it was harder to talk to Odette than anyone else. Whenever she entered the room, his words seemed to jumble in his throat, and he simultaneously wanted to be as far away from her and as close to her as possible. He didn't understand it, and the idea of exploring these emotions scared him.

"We—we didn't start," Bastian said. "Simon's just assembling the pages."

"Hi, Odette," Simon said.

"Hey, Simon." She took three strides across the room, tussled Callum's hair, and took a seat in the only other chair.

"Old lady," Callum said, grinning at her.

"Little boy," she said back to him.

Bastian smiled at their exchange. Odette was only two years older than Callum, but he came off as more immature in certain instances. All three of them, like many others, had arrived in 55178 at eight years old. Nobody remembered their lives before that. The three of them, Bastian, Callum, and Odette, considered each other best friends.

"Has Thayer connected anyone to *Water Bliss* yet?" Odette asked. She brushed at her freckled face, and Bastian forced himself to look away.

"Haven't talked to him," Callum said. "Hopefully, though. We sort of need water."

"All right," Simon said, standing up and moving his chair out of the way. "It's complete."

Bastian, Callum, and Odette moved closer to the desk. Spread across multiple pages all taped together was a drawing that made very little sense. Through their many secret meetings with Simon, he'd taught them how to decipher the first half of the picture. One piece of paper depicted fire and ash exploding out of mountains all over a blue-and-green planet. They'd never figured out whether that planet was the one they lived on or not.

Bastian scanned down the giant portrait, taking in all the information once more. On one piece of paper was an axe with blood dripping off its blade. Next to it, near the base of the axe's handle, was a small apple. Two interwoven snakes chasing each other's tails formed an eight next to the apple, and following that was the drawing of a giant stake in the ground. The number was indisputably 9.81.

The other drawings were of stars and planets. Simon fitted the new picture Bastian had found in the bottom. The page was still missing pieces, but it resembled a wheel with dozens of thick spokes so far.

"If someone is trying to send us a message," Odette said, biting her lip, "then why don't they just write one? Why be so cryptic?"

"They probably don't know if the person receiving these can read," Bastian said.

"He's right," Simon said, speaking past his knuckles. "Most residents of 55178 can't read. There's no necessity for it. That's why they're sending us drawings."

During his time stocking shelves, Bastian had learned to recognize essential words, most of them food related. It would also be hard to find someone who couldn't read the names of the Arcade games. Bastian assumed the lack of reading skills came from the inability to retrieve books. The Arcade games made it possible to retrieve anything necessary to their survival. Some of the games even went beyond that, providing ways to retrieve cards to play with and balls to kick around. Sure, most things—especially things like food, water, and medicine—dissolved after twenty-four hours, but at least one could enjoy them until then. But not all tools rusted and decayed—some things stayed, luckily. Bastian thought about how awful it would be if structures fell apart day after day.

Books arrived randomly and infrequently. Nobody asked for them, and nobody found them in the games. They would simply show up with other items in one of the Five Bins. Most of the time, the books contained instructions that helped with day-to-day life, but sometimes they were utter nonsense. Something called procreation, which never resulted in the women having babies. Bastian couldn't make sense of the half of it. A lot of the nonsense didn't apply to their life in 55178.

"I just don't know what they're getting at. Is this something that already happened or will happen? And the number." He pointed at the 9.81. "I've searched every book I could find in this town. As far as I can tell, it's non-sense."

"Maybe someone's pulling a prank on us," Callum

said. "One of the townsfolk or something. Maybe they're slipping the papers into the packaging when we're not looking."

"No," Simon said, eyes still on the diagram. "This is coming from out there." He made a general motion behind him, but everyone understood it to mean beyond the concrete walls.

"Why are you so convinced there's anything beyond those walls?" Callum asked.

Simon pressed his hands flat against his table and looked up slowly at him. "Don't you understand, boy? There *has* to be more to this life than playing games and barely surviving. Isn't it strange to you that none of us can remember our lives before we got here? Before we were eight years old?"

"Maybe that's just how the world works," Callum said, shrugging.

Simon shook his head but didn't speak further. Eventually, after everyone grew bored of the drawing, he said, "My XP is at 96. I can't get it to go any lower, and I'm not sure how much longer I can stall. The people are starting to notice that I'm not bringing in as much food as I used to."

Bastian's throat stiffened, and a dark feeling settled over his stomach. First Milt, and now Simon? How many more people would he have to lose?

"I want to find all the pieces to this drawing before I reach 100 XP," Simon said. "Before I Level Up."

"And if we figure out what this drawing means before then?" Bastian asked. He dared a glance at Odette. Her eyebrows were drawn together, and she was studying the drawing once more.

"I don't know," Simon said. "I don't know."

005:

The following day, Bastian, Callum, and Odette pushed their way inside the Arcade. For the second day in a row, it was jam-packed with people. All of them spoke with an air of excitement, and an unusual energy lifted Bastian's spirits. He'd felt abnormally down ever since Milt's sacrifice.

"He's bringing out the coin," Odette said. She was taller than Bastian by a couple of inches, and she had a better vantage point of *Water Bliss*. Bastian and Callum strained their necks, trying to see over the shoulders of the bustling townspeople.

Other gamers were at their own consoles, marquees glowing, heads wrapped in the rusty orange rubber caps. They swiveled joysticks and slammed buttons with hands covered in elbow-length gloves. *Doctor Bliss, Blissful Lumberjack, Blissful Pharmacy, Sewer Bliss*. There were dozens of games, and Bastian recognized all of them. Especially *Blissful Grocer*. Simon sat at that game, his eyes glued to the monitor, dark red hair covered by the rubber cap.

Bastian caught a glimpse of Thayer. He'd emerged from his room in the back and lumbered toward *Water Bliss,* hand held high, a silver coin pinched between his thumb and his finger.

"Haven't seen this many people at the spawning in a long time," Callum said, shrugging someone's sweaty hand off his shoulder.

"*Water Bliss* is one of the easier games," Odette explained. "And if you're chosen, it means instant popularity. People have to like the *Water Bliss* player. Without them, we wouldn't survive."

Bastian shouldered his way between two large people and made room for Callum and Odette. From this spot, they had a clear view of Thayer. He was a short man who seemed wider than he was tall. The most impressive red beard in all of 55178 belonged to Thayer. It reached all the way to his belt. The top of his head was bald and shining with sweat, but thick, curly red hair sprouted from the sides of his head, covering his ears.

Thayer reached down and slipped the coin into the coin slot. The monitor flickered, then revealed a plain blue screen. As though he'd practiced it a thousand times before, Thayer used the buttons to quickly tap up, up, down, down, left, right, left, right, red, blue, start. An influx of images rushed across the monitor. It was almost too fast to identify what they were, but Bastian knew they were photos of everyone in town, all two thousand of them.

Thayer pressed the red and blue buttons simultaneously, and the flashing images began swirling, disappearing deeper and deeper into the dark depths of the screen. Bastian held his breath, unsure whether he wanted to be chosen as the next *Water Bliss* gamer or not.

One picture appeared on the monitor. The crowd let out equal sighs of relief and of disappointment. Bastian squinted. The picture was of a woman he recognized from the other side of town. She was probably in her thirties. He didn't know her name.

"Kysee," Thayer said, using the name of the woman who'd just been chosen to be the next *Water Bliss* player. "Kysee?"

"She's not here," someone said.

"Go find her and tell her the news, then," Thayer responded, waving his hand.

"Well," Callum said quietly, "that was slightly disappointing."

Bastian agreed. Milt had hoped one of them would be chosen to play the game. But the wishes of dying men were rarely answered.

"Come on," Odette said, grabbing Bastian's hand. His heart stammered at the sudden contact, but he didn't pull away. It felt nice.

"I did it!"

Bastian flinched, and the departing townspeople turned to find the source of the noise. It was Dr. Soren. She was still seated at her console, but her balled fists were in the air, and her feet pounded the ground in quick succession.

"I finally did it!"

Dr. Soren removed her rubber cap and gloves and dropped them on the control panel of *Doctor Bliss*. In big, golden letters on her screen, it read: XP 100/100.

"I've Leveled Up," Dr. Soren said quietly, touching her lips as tears fell from her eyelids.

And there goes another one, Bastian thought.

Nobody congratulated Dr. Soren. They all knew what this meant. She would be gone forever by the end of the day. In the span of twenty-four hours, they'd lost two of their most essential gamers.

006:

As Dr. Soren ran out of the Arcade, nobody followed her. A few people said their goodbyes, tossing her happy, uncertain glances. She ignored most of them. Bastian, Callum, and Odette followed her. They'd never spoken it out loud, but all three of them found the Elevator fascinating, and they loved to see it operate.

It was an even hotter day than before. The sun was ruthless in its heat, and the concrete walls did nothing but add to it. The town itself seemed rather drab. There were no celebrations today, no sacrifices, no parties. There was no time for any of that. Dr. Soren was leaving, and today, the eight-year-olds showed up.

Bastian rubbed his wrist, following behind Odette and Callum, who were in deep conversation. He was tired, emotionally drained from the day before. He could see most of the town from this high up on the Arcade steps, and while the sight had captivated him as a child, it failed to do so now. He knew the names and purposes of all the square, flat buildings he saw, and for some reason, it all seemed less impressive than before.

The sky, a clear blue, showed no sign of clouds. It would be scorching hot all day long.

"Have the kids showed up yet?" Callum asked, glancing back at Bastian.

They'd descended to the bottom of the steps. They were the only people following Dr. Soren, who was almost jogging to the Elevator. Callum ran a hand through his hair, dark eyes watching Bastian expectantly.

"I think they came up early this morning, at least that's what Simon said. Fenna and Kace already took them to the condo."

Bastian remembered his first day ten years ago in 55178 as clearly as if it had been yesterday. He'd woken in an ascending metal box. Half an hour passed before the Elevator came to a stop. Then it had opened, revealing a world imprisoned by gargantuan stone walls and a blazing sun. A girl, who would later be named Polla, had ascended just minutes before him and seemed equally confused. The sun-baked concrete was the first thing he'd smelled, and then his life had begun.

He, too, had been taken to the condo, where he was raised by no one in particular, but watched over by Fenna and Kace until he turned twelve years old. Then he'd left the condo, found work with Simon, and lived in a small hut only two roads away from the grocery store.

Some years ago, he, Callum, and Odette had agreed to visit every new person who entered 55178 in hopes of making them feel more welcome. Even though Bastian and Callum were eighteen and Odette was twenty, they had all experienced that consuming loneliness. It was part of the reason they were such close friends.

As they passed the Five Bins, Bastian glanced at what had arrived already for the day ahead. A few younger kids had already gone through the effort to separate the items out into piles. One pile contained basic medical supplies: some orange tablets taken for body aches, packs of thick gauze, yellow bandages, and a syringe taped to a bottle of clear liquid. While all of this medicine would go bad in twenty-four hours just like everything else, Dr. Soren always stockpiled in case of emergencies. She detoured from her journey to the Elevator. The last thing Dr. Soren did for 55178 was to deliver the medical supplies to the infirmary.

Nobody wanted to wait a whole day for necessary medical equipment. Next to it, the children had filled water totes from the cistern. The water was still being rationed, but Bastian wasn't surprised. It was the woman, Kysee's, first day playing *Water Bliss*. It would take her a few days to figure out the game and start collecting the necessary water the town needed. Simon's pile, by far the largest, was a misshapen mound of tin boxes and cans. All of them were labeled. Bastian immediately started to mentally sort them out, calculating the amount of work he and Callum had later that day. The next two piles were much smaller. Obviously, not many people in the town had put in requests beyond food, which was good. It meant everybody was mostly satisfied.

The first of the last two piles was a simple tray with a dental drill and another syringe. Bastian cringed at the sight of it. He hated having his teeth worked on, and clearly, somebody needed a procedure done. The last pile was a huge stack of lumber. It wasn't sanded, but it was cut in even pieces. Bastian remembered that Garol, the town's lumberjack, had promised to build additional rooms at the condo, since it was apparently a little crowded.

Dr. Soren returned from the infirmary and sauntered to the waiting Elevator.

Bastian fidgeted when he bumped into Callum, who stood still next to Odette.

"You okay, Bastian?" Odette asked for the dozenth time that morning.

He nodded, annoyed by how distracted he was.

"Here goes nothing," Dr. Soren said, flashing a huge grin. Before her, only a few feet from the concrete wall, a hole in the ground opened. The Elevator—the same one that brought all the children up one by one—pushed up through the hole. It was a small square thing made from shiny metal. The two doors slid open, revealing one seat. Dr. Soren nearly jumped into the seat, unable to contain her excitement for the new chapter in life.

Bastian, Callum, and Odette peeked inside the Elevator. Nothing about it had changed since the last time they saw it. The walls were bare, and a seat made out of hard plastic was the only place to sit or stand inside. Dr. Soren hooped her legs through a safety harness, then pulled two belts over her shoulders and connected them to the harness's buckle. She was strapped in and ready to go.

"It's been a pleasure knowing all three of you," Dr. Soren said.

Bastian nodded, Callum waved, and Odette leaned in and wrapped the doctor in a quick hug.

"Hopefully, I'll see all of you again one day."

Odette stepped back. Her freckles were abundant in the stark sunshine.

The Elevator doors closed, and then it dropped back through the hole from which it had arrived. Seconds later, two metal doors slid over the open pit, sealing it shut.

"Wanna go check her vitals?" Callum asked. But it was a useless question. Bastian was already headed back to the Arcade.

007:

If Simon's office was considered an average size, then Thayer's was enormous. It could fit three times as many people as Simon's could. And his desk, made of polished, dark wood, was twice as big. On the wall above his desk were three giant screens, each one displaying photos of individuals from the town, their names, and their vital signs—EKG, pulse, blood pressure, and others.

Thayer sat in a high-back swivel chair. When Bastian, Odette, and Callum entered the office, he spun around.

"I noticed something *weird*," Thayer said. He pressed his glasses higher up on his nose and grinned. "*Weird weird.*"

He spun back around and pointed to the screen the farthest to the right. Using a white mouse, he navigated through an array of files on the computer, scrolling past hundreds and hundreds until he came across Dr. Soren's information.

Bastian wrinkled his nose. The office smelled faintly of salt and grease. It wasn't a bad smell, just unusual. Most residents of 55178 avoided food that doctors—specifically Dr. Soren—had warned them was bad for their health. Thayer, though, seemed to have disregarded those things entirely. He was definitely the biggest person in the town. His round belly pressed against the edge of the desk when he scooted in, and he'd long ago abandoned regular shoes for unprotective sandals. And while most people wore pants, Thayer wore shorts that ended just above his knees.

Food was portioned in 55178. While Simon tried to fulfill everyone's requests and collect it all in *Blissful Grocer,* he could seldom make everyone happy. He had to get a certain baseline amount every day to make sure nobody went hungry. Thayer, though, always got first dibs. It was part of the deal and why he had his hands on far more food than anyone else. Thayer was the only one capable of navigating the computer system, and it was always important to know the vitals of gamers, especially when they Leveled Up like Dr. Soren or were sacrificed like Milt.

"What do you have?" Bastian asked, leaning over Thayer's shoulder and looking up at the same screen he was.

"Well," Thayer said, grabbing a handful of some crunchy food from an open bag by his keyboard. "Remember when we talked about ATP?"

"No," Callum said, eyes drawn down.

"What do you mean no?" Odette asked. She turned to Callum, and her long hair whipped past Bastian's face. It smelled sweet, much better than his own hair, which currently smelled like sweat.

"I don't remember anything about ATP."

"I'm pretty sure you were here, Callum," Bastian said. "In fact, I distinctly remember you being here."

"I'm telling you," Callum said, lifting his hands to his head, "I don't remember anything about it."

"Probably wasn't listening," Thayer interjected. "Don't blame him. It's only the most interesting vital sign I monitor."

Callum shot Thayer an apologetic look, but Thayer ignored him. "Well, to refresh everyone here"—he eyed Callum—"ATP is an organic compound that happens within all of our bodies. It's technically called adenosine triphosphate, but that sounds gross to say, so we call it ATP. Anyway, ATP is what provides energy to our living cells. Without it, we wouldn't be able to grow. We'd all stay the same size we were as babies. Sound fun? No, to answer your question. No, it doesn't sound fun at all."

"And why is this interesting?" Callum asked.

"Bro," Bastian said, "can you focus for, like, five seconds?"

Odette chuckled, and Bastian had to hide his face in fear she'd see his cheeks go red.

"Our little monitors"—Thayer tapped his wrist in the same place Bastian could feel the unnatural bump on his—"the ones that read our vitals, they also measure our ATP. I never paid attention to it because it's not very important to us as a society, but when Dr. Soren reached 100 XP and her heart rate rose, I pulled up every one of her vitals. I have no idea why I did this. It sort of just happened."

He clicked a few more windows with his mouse and then pointed at two highlighted vitals listed next to a picture of Dr. Soren. One was her heart rate—which was a high 170. The other was her ATP levels.

"This is Dr. Soren's heart rate when she reached 100 XP. It's nothing to be alarmed about; this normally happens. Gamers get excited, and their heart rate goes through the roof. But her ATP is what has me concerned." He pointed at it. Bastian didn't understand what it meant, but he could read the numbers and letters—333.7 mol/L.

"I don't get it," Callum said. "Did I miss another conversation?"

"No," Thayer said. He moved to the monitor in the center and pulled up Bastian's profile. "Look at your levels, Bastian."

He did so, immediately recognizing how different they were. His ATP was .10 mol/L.

"Mine is much lower," he said. "Is there something wrong with me?"

"No," Thayer said, quickly dispelling any worries Bastian had. "Yours is perfectly normal. Most people's ATP levels are right around .10 mol/L. Dr. Soren's is just awfully high."

Bastian rubbed his chin. "I wonder what Milt's was like."

"I can tell ya," Thayer said, leaning over to a floor cabinet. "I print out vitals and keep them for a while."

"Why?" Callum asked.

Thayer shrugged. "I don't know. I just felt like I should. I only keep them for a few months." He licked his fat index finger and flipped through the pages. "Here his is."

"So Milt's never got that high," Bastian said.

"Interesting." Odette grabbed the paper.

Bastian looked over her shoulder and said, "It's not as high because he never Leveled Up, and at his age he never would have."

"Well, what do you think it means?" Odette asked.

"I don't know," Thayer admitted. "That's why I said it was weird. I'll keep looking into it. Hopefully, I find something to explain it all soon."

He swiveled back to face them, and Bastian blinked, taking his eyes off the glowing screens. The heat from outside was seeping through Thayer's walls, and Bastian had already begun sweating. Another blistering day.

Something beeped.

All eyes returned to the screens as the alarm continued. It wasn't deafening, but it was obnoxious. Bastian again leaned in close, the tufts of hair on the side of Thayer's head tickling his nose.

"That'd be Dr. Soren," Thayer said, pulling up her profile once again. Her vitals were far different than they had been moments ago. No longer did they display a random assortment of numbers. Instead, all her vitals were reporting a hollow, looming zero.

"That was fast," Odette said. "Less than an hour."

"What's the record again?" Callum asked. He picked at his fingernails, barely paying attention to what was going on in front of him. "I mean, the longest someone's vitals have kept going after they went down the Elevator."

"Fourteen hours," Thayer answered. He pressed his glasses up his nose again.

"It's good news, though," Odette said. "Now somebody else can link up to *Doctor Bliss*. We won't even have to go a day without medical supplies."

Thayer nodded, likely agreeing with what Odette was saying. But Bastian felt strange again. There was turmoil in his stomach. It was heavy and twisted, and it'd been growing since Milt's sacrifice. All these sacrifices, suspicious disappearances, and weird Arcade games . . . none of it felt right to Bastian.

He swallowed, pushing the feelings down. There would be time to sort through them later.

"Well," Callum said, "who wants to go haze a couple of new kids?"

008:

The view of the condo, a sprawling building of concrete and wood, brought Bastian both a sense of relief and a sense of uncertainty. He'd spent four years living within the walls of the building. And while it wasn't the first four years of his life, it was the first four years he remembered. He'd learned a lot about who he was and who he wanted to be behind those walls. He'd met Odette and Callum during playtime. He'd done almost all his growing up at the condo, and it provided him a heavy dose of nostalgia. At the same time, the building made him slightly uneasy. He'd feared the condo—and 55178 in general—throughout his entire first year, and though he'd tried, he'd never been able to fully shake that feeling.

Shortly after leaving Thayer's, Bastian had remembered that he and Callum still had to organize the grocery store for Simon. They'd said a temporary goodbye to Odette and then had done just that. Once their jobs at the grocery store were finished—and having found no new mysterious scraps of paper—they'd found Odette at her home and immediately set off for the condo.

Night had fallen an hour previous and brought with it a requisite, exquisite coolness. The moon was at its fullest, a shining orb directly above them, and provided so much light that the three had no issues navigating the cobblestone streets. They could even see the condo from here. It stood taller than most buildings and was only a ten-minute walk away.

"What do you think their names are?" Callum asked, skipping ahead of Bastian and Odette and then walking backward, so he faced them.

"I'm sure Kace and Fenna haven't named them yet," Odette said, giving him her signature "older sister" look.

"You think they'll let us pick their names?"

"I doubt it," Bastian said. "Especially considering what kind of names you'd give them."

"Ooh," Odette said, her dimples deepening when she smiled. "Do tell me what kind of names you have in mind, Callum."

"Trust me," Bastian said, "they're worse than the worst names you can imagine."

Odette scrunched up her nose and sneered at Callum. "Try me, little boy."

"All right, well," Callum began as they turned onto Daed Street. "Let me think."

Here, the buildings were closer together, and all resembled the same pattern—boxy, a door on the front, and two windows on either side. They were all painted different shades of blue. Occasionally, Bastian would look through the windows of the homes and spot a couple at the dinner table or a kid his age eating alone. He wondered if people ever watched him when he wasn't looking.

"Okay, I think I've got it," Callum continued. "Are you sure you're ready for this, old lady?"

Odette shrugged, nudging Bastian with her shoulder. He got the hint and focused on Callum.

"Fenna and Kace name the kids whatever they want now, and that's that, no further discussion. Well, I think names need to *mean* something. Do you understand?"

"Sure do," Odette said. Bastian nodded along with her.

Callum looked over his shoulder, checked that the road was clear, and continued his backward stroll. "I think, to make it easier, we should name people after what they're wearing when they arrive in the Elevator."

Odette raised her eyebrows, then stared at Bastian with her huge blue eyes. "Is he serious?" she whispered.

"I told you it was really bad," he said, laughing.

"Like, if somebody arrived in a gray shirt," Callum continued, "that's what we'd call them. Gray Shirt. Or Red Pants. No Shoes. Broken Belt. You get the idea."

Odette laughed, the sound catching in her throat and making her snort. "I'm sorry, Callum," she said, still giggling, "but that's really dumb."

"No, listen, hear me out. I know it sounds dumb, *but* it's the only thing we bring with us from"—Callum waved his hands at the giant concrete walls partially hidden by the darkness—"out there."

"Ah-ha!" Bastian shouted, springing forward, finger pointed at Callum. "So you *do* admit you think there's something beyond these walls!"

"I never said I didn't," Callum said, running both his hands through his hair.

"Nah, buddy," Odette interjected, "you can't get away with this one. I was there last night when you pretty much said you don't think there's anything past these walls."

"See?" Bastian said, fist-bumping Odette. "The old lady backs me up!"

"Fine!" Callum shouted, throwing his hands down to his sides. "You caught me. Yeah, I think something exists beyond these walls. I'm not an idiot. Obviously, all these eight-year-olds come from somewhere. Obviously, *we* came from somewhere. And babies, in the medical books. We can't have any, and trust me, I've heard people try. But I don't really understand the point of worrying about it. We've all tried blasting a hole, digging under the walls, and even scaling them. I mean, everyone in 55178 tried scaling the walls a few years back, but we all know it's impossible. There's nothing in this entire town that can get us over those walls. So I've just stopped worrying about it. I don't think we'll ever find out where we came from."

A moment of silence passed between the three. Callum spun on his heel and continued down the path to the condo. Bastian bowed his head, mulling over Callum's words. Maybe he was right, maybe Bastian was just wasting his energy worrying about whether there was more to life.

"You give up too easy," Odette said, making both boys pause. "There's gotta be a way past these walls. And if anybody is ever gonna find it, it'll be us."

009:

The condo was swarming with activity.

It was a giant building. Aside from children's drawings hanging in some of the windows, little had been done to make the outside appear welcoming. The yard was well manicured, though the grass had browned years ago, since in years past, Milt's ability to play for excess water had diminished, and now thoughtfully placed rocks made up the space. It still looked nice, though.

Kids ran about the lawn, screaming and kicking and laughing. Many of them were sunburned but didn't seem to mind. Bastian knew all of their names. He'd made an effort to and was proud of it.

Bastian led Odette and Callum to the front door. He didn't knock and instead went inside without an invitation. None of the kids paid them any attention, too focused on their games.

The interior of the condo was much more comforting than the exterior. Here, Fenna and Kace had gone to extraordinary lengths to set it apart from the other buildings. They'd lined the concrete beams with wood panels, carpeted the ground, and added shelves on every wall that they'd covered with toys, trophies, and art. It was lit by candles as well. Bastian didn't know why Fenna and Kace had stopped using electrical light years before; he'd never asked.

The front door led to a lobby with half a dozen chairs. They passed through that and made it to the massive dining room. A few kids sat at the unusually long table, scrawling things onto the paper before them, and paid Bastian and his friends no attention when they entered.

"Bastian!" It was Fenna. She strode forward in a robe and grabbed Bastian by the cheeks. "It's so good to see you." She kissed him on his forehead and gripped him in a tight hug. When she pulled away, she hugged Callum and Odette, whispering their names and kissing them too.

"We came by to see the new kids," Bastian said, pointing to the corridor leading away from the dining room.

"They're good kids," Fenna said, smiling. She was a plain woman with curled red hair that stopped just above her ears. Her nose came to a sharp point. "Really great. A boy and a girl, as usual. I hear Dr. Soren Leveled Up today, which means we should be getting two more kids tomorrow."

"She did," Bastian said. "Vitals flattened really quick."

"Do you have enough room for two more?" Odette asked.

"Kace is helping Garol finish another section of the building, and then we should. Besides, in a few months, nearly ten kids are aging out, so we'll lose all of them."

Bastian remembered the day he had turned twelve, how anxious he'd been about leaving the condo, how his entire future had been unknown. He empathized with the grown kids who were expected to soon survive independently, but he also understood it was necessary, so the younger children had someplace to stay. To this day, six years later, he still felt like he was lost in limbo. His responsibilities at the grocery store had come by accident. His friendships with Simon, Thayer, the Leveled-Up Dr. Soren, and the late Milt weren't sought out by any of them. He had simply spent each day surviving until one day it wasn't just survival, just coping, it was actual living.

He still wasn't satisfied, not entirely. His wish to find out what was beyond the concrete walls of 55178 was much stronger than he let on. He dreamed about it at night, of what the rest of the sky looked like. He dreamed of the possibility of towns just like 55178 next to them, filled with similar, red-haired people. Maybe there, they didn't play Arcade games for survival; perhaps they played board games, or trivia games, or solved puzzles.

Or maybe, Bastian thought, *they don't play any games at all. Maybe they hunt for their own food.*

He'd thought about that before. Although nobody had a clue who designed the Arcade games, their logic was far too consistent to be a coincidence. This was how people long ago survived, people generations before Bastian arrived, before the Arcade was built. Or maybe people did exist beyond the walls, and the Arcade games were based on their real-life actions. Instead of playing a game collecting water from a river like Milt, they *actually* had to avoid tigers to collect water from a river.

The smell of beans and toast permeated the air. The scent of the stale food had somehow overpowered the candles. It wasn't pleasant, but nobody complained.

"We'd like to meet them," Odette said. She glanced at Bastian, lowering her eyebrows, asking him a silent question. He nodded to her, letting her know he was okay.

"Of course," Fenna said. "I believe they're helping Kace and Garol. Follow me."

010:

The condo seemed even larger on the inside. Since most of the square footage came from additions made over the years, it was more of a maze than a proper building. When Bastian was younger, it had made for killer games of Piggy Want a Wave, but as he navigated it now, he was far too busy trying to map it out in his head.

"You cannot name them," Odette told Callum as they followed Fenna through hallways and rooms. Everywhere they went, there were children. Most paid little attention to the trio, though a few shouted their names, ran to them, quickly hugged them, then scampered off.

"Why not?" Callum asked. "Fenna said they don't have names yet. Why shouldn't I get to name a couple?"

"Because your names are stupid, little boy," she said.

Callum sighed, then stormed ahead of Odette, joining Fenna.

"Is everything okay?" Odette asked Bastian moments later.

"Yeah," he said, without actually considering the question. "Why do you ask?"

She paused as if she, too, had not considered the question before asking it. "You seem really distracted lately. Ever since Milt was sacrificed, I can't really seem to get your full attention."

He looked at her then, meeting her dazzling blue eyes, her freckles faint in the dim lighting of the condo. "I'm sorry," he told her. His eyes settled on her lips, and a throbbing started in his chest, a deep ache he had yet to resolve. When she responded, he nearly forgot to listen to her. He was too distracted by the way the shadows brightened her eyes and how her fair skin seemed entirely unblemished when passing by the flame of a candle.

"As long as everything's okay," she said as they came upon a vast, open room in the condo. When Odette caught him looking at her, she smiled, her cheeks reddening. "What?"

Without answering, he ducked through the doorway after Callum and Fenna, leaving Odette standing on the other side, confused.

Kace and Garol were both burly men who possessed features the other one was missing. Kace had a full head of auburn hair, and his face was clean-shaven. Garol had a long and bushy beard, but his head was as bald as concrete. The two had so far assembled a wall out of the long, sturdy planks of wood and were currently using a screwdriver to attach sheetrock to the boards.

Two kids, obviously eight years old, stood near Kace and Garol, holding buckets of tools and screws. The girl's hair went down to her waist and was tangled and ratty, as if it hadn't been brushed in a few days. She wore an oversized green T-shirt. The boy had a buzz cut—just like Bastian—and wore boots far too big for his feet.

"Hello," Callum said, approaching the kids. They turned to face him, eyes widening in concern. "My name is Callum." He bent down so he was eye-level with them. "Your names are Green Shirt and Big Boots."

"All right!" Odette shouted. She strode past Bastian and Fenna and went to Callum and the kids.

"Hey, Fenna!" Kace said, using his drill to screw the final corner of sheetrock into the wood. "Bastian." He placed his tools on the ground and approached them.

"Came to meet the kids," Bastian said, pointing to the eight-year-olds.

"Well," Kace said, his voice gruff and scratchy. "I won't take offense to that. It's nice to see you too, Bastian." Bastian smiled and shook his hand. The man had an unnervingly firm grip that always managed to hurt his knuckles.

"How's the condo?" Bastian asked.

"Wonderful," Kace said. "After years and years, we finally have a pretty decent schedule down. Fenna has even started some of the kids on learning."

"Really?" Bastian asked, raising his eyebrows.

"Some of them can already read better than me," Kace said, jabbing his thumbs at himself. "Mighty impressive, I say."

"Well," Bastian said, "we need more people in this town who can read." He thought of Simon's collection of drawings, how they believed someone had sent them a message in pictures instead of words. Maybe the residents of 55178 weren't supposed to be capable of reading, but a few had somehow learned over the years.

"How's working for Simon?" Kace asked. Fenna shook her head at his question, but Bastian didn't understand why.

"The usual," Bastian said, pulling at the collar of his brown shirt. "It keeps Callum and me busy, so we're happy to do it."

Kace nodded and met Fenna's gaze. She coughed, and then he looked around awkwardly, as if he was afraid somebody was standing too close.

"Listen," Kace said, leaning in close to Bastian, "Fenna has been—" She nudged him, and he inhaled sharply. "Okay. Fenna *and I* have been meaning to ask you something."

"Go ahead," Bastian said. He looked at Odette and Callum, who both knelt by the new kids. They were mostly just listening now. The children had opened up and were jabbering their ears off. Garol continued with the wall, now taping the seams of the sheetrock.

"Has he been telling you any weird things?" Kace asked. "Like, conspiracies and such? We've heard some of the young kids talking about hidden messages and stuff beyond the walls." His voice had lowered to a hoarse whisper. "Do you know anything about that?"

At first, Bastian didn't respond. His heart had dropped in his chest, and he felt the sweat on his hands. Clearly, Kace was referring to the drawings Bastian and Callum were helping Simon find, the ones depicting the exploding mountains, the stars, and the strange spoke-thing they had yet to identify. While they had never technically agreed to keep it a secret, there'd always been an unspoken rule to do so. People in 55178 didn't react kindly to speculation. For whatever reason, conspiracy theories and discussions about what was beyond the concrete walls were always met with alarm.

"No," Bastian said, his voice catching in his throat. "He hasn't told me anything."

Fenna nodded, accepting Bastian's lie. "I, for one, find it inappropriate. He shouldn't be indoctrinating innocent children with his weird beliefs."

"Fenna wants to talk to him," Kace explained. She

nudged him again, and he groaned. "Fenna wants *me* to talk to him. Tell him it's fine to think the things he does, but he shouldn't be speaking those thoughts out loud."

Bastian nodded. Was what he, Odette, and Callum were doing wrong? If they were caught, would they be held responsible for some sort of crime? He didn't think so, but he didn't know for sure.

"I'll let you know if I hear anything," Bastian said in the calmest tone he could manage.

"Thank you," Fenna said. Kace just nodded.

"Odette, Callum," Bastian said. The two looked at him, turning away from the babbling children. "We have to go. I forgot about that second run Simon made on *Blissful Grocer.* We never put it on the shelves."

Callum and Odette eyed him with a palpable amount of suspicion, but neither raised their concerns. They said goodbye to the children, promised to visit soon, then began to leave.

"Better hurry," Fenna said, giving him a warm smile. "Don't want perfectly good food to rot so soon."

011:

Bastian, Callum, and Odette left the condo in silence. Bastian ignored their lingering stares, focusing on slowing his racing heart. Once they were well out of earshot of Kace, Fenna, and all of the children, he rounded the corner of the nearest concrete building and pressed his back against the wall.

"What's going on?" Odette asked, throwing her hands in the air, her eyes darting about wildly. Bastian had never seen her like this. Was she scared? He didn't know she was capable of being afraid.

"Fenna and Kace know about Simon's theories," Bastian said. He slid to the ground, pulling his knees up to his chest.

"And?" Callum asked.

"And they seem really upset about it."

"That's what you're worried about?" Odette asked. "Jeez, Bastian. You seemed so worried. I thought something bad had happened." She pressed her hand against her chest and took two deep breaths.

"Yeah, why are you so worried about it?" Callum asked.

But Bastian didn't have an answer. Now that he reflected on the situation, he realized that he had no reason to be concerned, no reason to be upset. It wasn't unnatural for citizens of 55178 to be wary of conspiracy theories, especially when the speculation went to the unknown beyond the concrete walls. Fenna and Kace hadn't posed any sort of threat. They'd just been concerned about certain information making the rounds in the town. They were probably just trying to protect their children from rumors they thought were false.

"I don't know," Bastian admitted. "I just got a weird vibe from it all."

"Weird vibes or not," Odette said, "maybe we should just keep denying that Simon has told us anything. He's our friend, and I think we owe him at least that much."

✳✳✳

Bastian lay in bed, eyes wide open, staring into the darkness of the room. He and Callum shared a small home on the opposite side of town from the Arcade. It'd taken them a while to snag it; it'd been owned by a man named Akob, who played *Blissful Apparel,* the game that allowed the residents to get clothes—not that any of them ever fit well. About six years previous, he'd Leveled Up, and Bastian and Callum had immediately laid claim on his home.

While Bastian wasn't one who yearned to be without company, he found the loneliness of night to be a comforting thing. It was the only time of day he truly had to himself, and he spent more of it spinning scenarios in his own head than he cared to admit.

His bed creaked when he rolled over, the mattress

springs pressing into his ribs. He fluffed his pillow, growing slightly frustrated that it was nearly impossible to find a comfortable place to sleep—55178 was not conducive to comfort.

Why had he been nervous when Fenna and Kace had asked him about Simon? Was it the tone of their voices, the specific words they used, their body language? Was it because he was uncomfortable with Simon's conspiracy theories and the picture he was assembling from secret papers found in the food deliveries? He didn't think so. None of those answers made sense to him. And yet, he couldn't shake that feeling of unease. *Something* was off about the whole situation—he just didn't know what.

And then there was Odette. She'd seemed so scared when Bastian had pulled them away from the condo. Callum hadn't acted frightened, but Odette had nearly been petrified. Why? There was no logical reason for her to have reacted that way.

He decided, after some thought, that Odette's reaction was born from one of two reasons. One, she knew or suspected something Bastian didn't that frightened her— something that was weighing on her mind. The second reason seemed much less realistic to Bastian, though he secretly wished it were true. Maybe Odette cared about Bastian, and she'd been scared because she was hyper-aware of him. Perhaps she got that same anxious feeling in her stomach when she saw him like he did with her.

When he thought about that, his stomach churned, and it threatened to upheave everything within if he encouraged those thoughts any further. So he shifted to another topic: the walls.

He knew without a doubt that there was something beyond the concrete walls. Even if most people didn't like to discuss it, he thought they also knew the same thing.

This world didn't make sense. The town was built to run on Arcade games, played by people who were delivered as eight-year-olds through the Elevator hidden in the ground. He had no doubt in his mind that there was more to the world than 55178.

Eventually, he fell into a fitful sleep, where he dreamed about giant human beings that existed beyond the concrete walls. When Bastian woke up hours later, the blazing sun trying to burn a hole through his windowpanes, he had a new thought.

Maybe the walls weren't there to keep the residents in 55178. Maybe the walls were there to keep something out.

012:

For the second morning in a row, Bastian found himself crammed shoulder-to-shoulder in the Arcade. He sighed in annoyance. Usually, people didn't attend spawnings, but for some reason, they'd felt the need to attend the one held for *Water Bliss,* and now the one for *Doctor Bliss.* It probably had something to do with Milt and Dr. Soren, two people who'd been in 55178 almost longer than anyone.

After a slightly miserable night's sleep, Bastian found the conversation with Kace and Fenna about Simon less strange than it had felt the day before. There was still some instinct deep within him sending off warning signals, but he couldn't identify them. Whatever was off about the entire situation remained hidden to him.

"Man, people are itching for something new," Callum said, scratching his head.

"I see Thayer," Odette said, pointing near the back of the Arcade. Her freckles were invisible in the Arcade's soft lighting, and her usual bright red hair was a burnt orange.

"He's brought the silver coin," Odette said, narrating the event to Bastian and Callum.

A chatter of excitement rippled through the crowd. Callum was right. People just wanted something new, something mildly interesting to help them through the drab and dull days.

"He's doing the thingy now," Odette said.

"What thingy?" Callum asked.

"Where he wiggles the joystick and presses all the buttons. I don't know. The thingy."

Bastian recognized the familiar whirr of the machine, indicating the pictures of all the town's residents were flying up onto the monitor. The crowd was captured by a sudden silence, and then the entire room shifted. It was as if the walls pressed together all at once and forced everyone's attention to something in the center of the crowd.

"Odette," Bastian said, "who is it?"

But Odette didn't answer. She was frozen, stiff, her usual cheery face now a shade grayer. Bastian reached out to her, grabbing her by the wrist. There was no flutter in his stomach this time, no patter of his heart. Her skin felt cold.

"Odette," Callum said, nudging her with his elbow.

A chill ran through Bastian's body. "Odette, who is it?" But he already knew the answer.

"Odette!" Thayer shouted from the *Doctor Bliss* machine. "Odette!"

Bastian's hopes sank. He hadn't realized until just then how he'd always secretly hoped neither he, Callum, nor Odette would be picked for one of the Arcade games. Ever since they arrived here, they were taught that winning the spawning was an honor, something to look forward to. But Bastian had never felt that way about the games. Yes, if chosen, you were able to provide necessities to the town, you were able to help them survive, but there was more to it than that. Becoming a gamer didn't just come with responsibilities. It also came with expectations. You were no longer supposed to just complete your tasks for the town. As a gamer, you were expected to go above and beyond. If Odette underperformed, the town would take it out on her.

Not only that, but now Odette was, essentially, a celebrity. Within a few days, everybody would know Dr. Odette, the *Doctor Bliss* gamer. She would have considerably less time to spend with Bastian and Callum.

Will she have time for us at all? Bastian thought, the feeling creating a deep sense of dread within him.

"Odette," Thayer said. Bastian looked up. The crowd had parted. A clear path had been formed between Odette and *Doctor Bliss*. She swallowed hard, eyeing it with eyes that didn't seem to be seeing anything at all. Then, with another nudge from Callum, she took one step forward. Bastian's hand fell loose from her wrist, and she took one quick glance back at him.

"If you're okay with it," Thayer said, "we'll connect you right now. If not, we can wait until fewer people are around."

Odette shook her head, every ounce of her bubbly personality now void. She was a statue of her former self.

"No," she said, her voice dry. "Get it over with."

Thayer guided her to the stool that, one day earlier, had been occupied by Dr. Soren. Once she sat down, Thayer produced the elbow-length, rust-colored gloves. He held them out to her, and she fit her hands inside slowly. Then Thayer pulled the rubber cap off the top of the cabinet where a thick black wire, about the girth of an adult male's arm, ran up through the ceiling. He drew the cap down on her head, its many wires like the hairs of a robotic creature, the small bulbs lining the edge like unblinking eyes. He fit it over Odette's head, pushing down what little fluff was in her hair.

"All good?" Thayer asked.

Bastian couldn't see Odette's face from where he stood, so he had no idea what she whispered to Thayer. But then Thayer moved around the machine and flicked a switch. The entire cabinet shut down, the screen with Odette's face going completely black. Even the light illuminating the marquee went dark. Then, just as quickly, the machine powered on.

Odette flinched.

Before he knew what he was doing, Bastian was at Odette's side. Her eyes were shut, and her pale cheeks were wet with tears. He grabbed her gloved hand.

"Are you okay?" he asked her.

"I'm fine," she said, opening her eyes. "Didn't hurt all that much. Just scared, that's all."

Bastian smiled, trying to project a sense of comfort, but he knew he had failed. He felt even more uneasy than during his conversation with Kace and Fenna, and he suspected Odette shared that same feeling. Something was wrong, and while he still couldn't pinpoint where that feeling originated from, he was wary. And judging by the look on Odette's face, she was too.

"You're officially connected," Thayer said, reemerging from behind the machine. He shooed his hands at the crowd, and they murmured, leaving slightly disgruntled. "Nobody requested medical supplies today, so you're not due on the game until tomorrow."

"Okay," Odette said as Callum appeared at her other side.

"Welcome to the Arcade, Dr. Odette."

013:

By the time they got to the cafeteria, most of the residents had already eaten their lunch. It was yet another concrete structure across the street from the Arcade. Inside, a portion of the building was sectioned off for the storage and preparation of food. The rest was a massive open space with dozens upon dozens of tables, all situated in neat rows.

Bastian, Callum, and Odette sat in one of the corners. A couple hundred other individuals were gathered at their own tables, but they were far enough away that Bastian paid them no attention.

Callum had devoured his can of beans nearly half an hour ago, but Bastian and Odette continued to slowly pick away at theirs. None of them had opened their can of vegetables. At this point in their lives, they could barely stomach the thought of them—though they eventually forced them down when ravenous hunger drove them to it.

"If there is anything on the . . ." Callum looked around to ensure no one was within hearing distance before whispering, ". . . *other side,* do you think they eat more than just beans and greens?"

"We eat more than just beans and greens," Bastian said. "You literally had cake for breakfast."

Odette chuckled, and some weight fell off Bastian's shoulders. It was the first sign of normalcy she'd shown since winning the spawning.

"Yeah, but how often do we get cake?" Callum asked. "Our diet consists mostly of beans and greens. Sometimes we get good cereal, occasionally we get a dinner that doesn't taste like tin, and rarely do we ever get dessert. And if Simon does manage to snag us some good food from *Blissful Grocer,* we have to eat it immediately, or it rots within twenty-four hours."

"We know how it works," Bastian said. He was growing annoyed with Callum's careless attitude. While he usually appreciated it, he thought it might offend Odette, who had yet to say a word since they'd left the Arcade.

"Well, I don't care. I'm just wondering whether you think food is different on the outside?"

Bastian pinched his nose. There was a faint odor of rot here. It was impossible to avoid since nearly everything delivered through the Five Bins rotted or dissolved within a day. He was just thankful he'd landed the stocking job, and not the *other* shift. Clearing out racks of rotten food every day had to wear on a person. Not that Bastian was completely shielded from it. The bin behind the grocery store was supposed to empty somewhere below, but it only did so when it was completely full.

"It has to be," Bastian said. "Right? Everything has to be better."

And then he remembered his dream from the night before and how it led him to wonder for the first time whether the concrete walls were there to keep them prisoners or there to keep them safe.

"Or maybe not," he added.

"I think it's better," Odette said. She looked at the ground. A bit of color had returned to her face, and Bastian even spotted the freckles dotting her cheeks. "Anything would be better than this." Then she pressed her hand to her forehead and began to cry.

Bastian looked up at Callum, whose eyes immediately grew so wide, it looked like they'd nearly pop out. He motioned toward Odette, hissing unintelligible words at Bastian.

Confused by Callum's nonsensical movements and overwhelmed by Odette's crying, Bastian froze halfway between wrapping his arm around Odette and leaving the table.

Before he could make a decision, Callum grabbed his unopened can of vegetables and stood up. "I think these greens will taste better if I eat them outside."

Then Callum was gone so fast that Bastian was convinced he'd disappeared into thin air.

So instead of leaving the table, Bastian wrapped his arm around Odette. She leaned into him, covering her entire face with both her hands, continuing to cry. She felt warm against his side, her long hair soft on his arms.

"I'm sorry," he said.

"I just—don't know—what I'm doing," she said between sobs.

"I'm sure you'll figure it out," Bastian said. He looked over his shoulder, searching desperately for anyone who seemed more capable of comforting a crying woman than him, but the remaining citizens had left the cafeteria. It was empty, hollow, nothing but echoes.

"You have Callum and me," he said, rubbing her arm

with his hand, "and we'll do anything we can to help. I'm also sure Thayer and Simon will teach you how to play the game. Really, it's going to be okay."

Odette wiped at her eyes, swallowing and sniffling, then pulled away from Bastian's embrace. Her cheeks were red, and her eyes shimmered with unshed tears, but she sat up straight anyway.

"You're right," she said. "I'm sure this is how everybody feels when they win the spawning." She wiped her wet hands on her pants, patched with all the different colors of fabric, then let out a long sigh.

"Thank you," she said.

"I didn't really do anything," he said, trying to shake the awkwardness of the compliment.

"You stayed with me. That means a lot." She wiped again at her eyes, removing the last few trickling tears.

"Yeah, sorry about Callum."

"He shouldn't have to comfort a crying old lady." She smiled at her own joke, and Bastian smiled too, though he was still on edge, paranoid that she would erupt into a geyser of tears at any moment.

"Dr. Odette?"

The voice came from the entrance to the cafeteria. Both Bastian and Odette whirled around, startled by the noise, but relaxed when they saw Mira, the librarian, approaching them.

Mira was an elderly lady who claimed she was a hundred years old. While many people doubted that was her actual age, nobody could deny it. She'd been around longer than anyone. Her red hair had long ago turned into a stark gray, and she kept it long. It fell past her shoulders, loose and free. She began hobbling over to Bastian and Odette, using a cane to support her steps. In her free hand, she held a gray book.

Once she had crossed the room, she took a seat next to Odette. She was dressed in the usual: a nightgown that brushed her ankles and the softest pair of slippers in 55178. Bastian remembered the moment five years ago when Mira had publicly and loudly declared during lunch that she was done with the "drab clothes" and would be wearing pajamas for the rest of her life.

"You did win the spawning today, right?" she asked, her voice rattling.

"Yes, ma'am," Odette said.

"Good, thought maybe I got the wrong Odette." She smiled, some of the wrinkles on her cheeks disappearing momentarily. Then she held up the gray book and pressed it into Odette's hands.

"This is everything you'll need to know about medicine and medical procedures," Mira said. She pressed her half-moon spectacles up her nose. "I've given this book to all the people who played *Doctor Bliss*. And when I heard Dr. Soren had Leveled Up, I went to her place and immediately took this back before anyone else could."

Odette stared at the book, running her hand along its blank cover.

"You can read, right?" Mira asked.

Both Bastian and Odette nodded.

"Good," Mira said, scratching her wrist. "Every doctor for the last nine decades has learned from this book. Study it, and you won't have a problem at all."

Then, using her cane, Mira lifted herself from the table seat and hobbled back the way she'd come.

"See?" Bastian asked, giving Odette one more hug. "I told you it'll all be okay."

014:

After lunch, Odette retired to her home to study the book Mira had given her, and Bastian had left to find Callum. For some reason, Simon had gotten a late start on *Blissful Grocer,* so Bastian and Callum had to work later than usual. Neither of them particularly minded. Most evenings, they struggled to find entertaining ways to spend their time. Working kept them busy.

Today's haul was bigger than normal, and Bastian didn't really understand why. Simon had been hovering around 96 XP for a while. He even started bringing in a little less food as of late, so he didn't gain any experience points. While Bastian wasn't entirely clear on the details, he understood that all of the Arcade games were programmed into Thayer's vitals monitors, so the games were always aware of how much the town needed in regard to food, clothing, medicine, and other necessities. If someone collected the required items, their XP would slowly rise throughout the years. If they collected less, it would neither increase nor lower. But the more time they spent playing the game, and the more items they ordered, the higher their XP climbed.

Like any other gamer, Simon had once been dead set on reaching 100 XP and Leveling Up. But when he, Bastian, and Callum began finding the drawings in the food tins, his entire attitude had changed. He'd become obsessed with completing the drawing and solving the puzzle, so he'd begun underperforming in the game. It'd been nearly six months, and he hadn't raised a single point in XP.

"Do you think Odette's gonna be okay?" Callum asked. He stood at the end of the dimly lit aisle next to a mound of packaged food. His movements of placing them on the shelves were methodical, as if he'd entered a trance. His red hair fell down his face in thick, shadowy tendrils. If Bastian didn't know him better, the whole sight would feel way more ominous than it was.

"She'll be fine," Bastian said, even though he wasn't sure he believed it. "Odette's the smartest person I know. Once she plays the game and realizes she's more than capable, I think she'll calm down about the whole thing."

"Ah," Callum said, and then he sat down on the floor.

"Tired?" Bastian asked.

"Not really. Just thinking." He paused for a moment as Bastian placed canned greens on the shelf. The tin was cool to his fingers—an odd sensation considering 55178 was blanketed by an eternal, blistering heat.

"Do you ever think you'll win the spawning?" Callum asked.

The question made Bastian hesitate. It had never really occurred to him before that morning. He wondered how he'd react. Would he be like Odette? Scared, unsure, depressed? Or would he be like Simon, who apparently had screamed with joy when he'd won the spawning? He wasn't sure. The idea of playing one of the Arcade games was exciting simply because it was new. He'd never played one before, and it would be a nice break from stocking shelves. But winning the spawning came with a price. He'd be tied to that game for the rest of his life. The expectations placed upon him would be nauseating. He would never, ever get a break because the town would never, ever go without needing.

"I hope not," Bastian answered, and he believed himself that time.

Bastian picked up another cereal box and jumped at the familiar *tink tink* of a paperclip within. He popped open the box, pulled out the foil bag containing the cereal, and then dumped the item into his hand. This time, it wasn't a scrap of paper attached to a paperclip that fell out of the box. This time, it was an *entire page*.

He stared at it, slightly dumbstruck. He struggled to make sense of the drawing, though it definitely belonged with the picture Simon had been assembling for months. Was this the final piece? When combined with the rest, would the puzzle finally form a cohesive image and make sense?

"Whoa," Callum said.

"Whoa, indeed," Bastian replied, abandoning his pile of food in the middle of the aisle and making his way to the office in the back.

Simon gamed for roughly four hours in the morning. The food was delivered almost instantaneously once he finished, and while Bastian and Callum stocked the shelves, Simon spent that time consolidating the requests from the town into spreadsheets and planning his path through the next day's game.

Bastian entered without knocking.

Simon spun around in his swivel chair. His red hair

was, like always, parted to the left, and splotches of sweat stains spotted his black hoodie.

"Did you find—" He froze when he saw Bastian, his ecstatic grin immediately forming into a giant O shape.

"Whoa," he whispered, staring at the drawing Bastian held.

"Whoa, indeed," Bastian replied.

015:

"What the heck is Simon up to?" Callum asked as he and Bastian crept down another alley. The sun had long ago buried itself behind the looming concrete walls, taking most of its heat with it. Now, the stars were out, and the moon was as bright as always. The night air brought with it a biting chill; it was one of the rare occasions Bastian wished he had a coat. Instead, he and Callum had taken their blankets and wrapped them around themselves, giving their bare arms some warmth.

Bastian pressed himself against the wall, holding the blanket together at his neck. A plume of frosty air ballooned out of his mouth, and he shivered at the sight of it. They stood below a window looking into one of the many apartments lining Alus Street. Most residents had shut off their lights and gone to bed for the night, but a few shining windows still penetrated the moonlit darkness. Bastian looked about the alley, glancing left and right down the street, then turned back to face Callum.

"Dude!" Callum hissed. "What're we doing?"

"I don't know," Bastian said. His hands shook, either

from his nerves or the cold. "When I showed Simon the drawing I found today, he took it from me and told me to go home with you and not come back until midnight."

"So why are we sneaking around like a couple of suspicious weirdos?"

"He told me to make sure we weren't followed."

"See?" Callum said. "All I needed was an explanation. You would have saved so much breath if you'd just let me in on the reasons behind our late-night excursion."

"Will you shut up?" Bastian asked, a flare of anger temporarily warming his stomach. He returned his attention to the street. It was still vacant of all activity. "I think we're clear, but we need to run."

Without waiting for a response, Bastian bolted from the alley, his blanket flailing out behind him like a cape. His worn shoes thudded the pavement as he careened past the Arcade. Behind him, he heard Callum, whose feet seemed to be far heavier and much louder than his.

When they reached the grocery store, Bastian only spotted one window where light shone through. It was across the street, in the living room of a small home. He squinted but saw nothing more. If somebody was watching them, they would have no idea.

Bastian ripped open the door to the store and darted inside, Callum only two feet behind him. When it shut behind them, Callum locked it, and then the two of them went down the aisles, passing their unkempt piles of food.

The door to Simon's office was locked. Before Bastian could knock, Simon opened it from the other side.

"Come in," he whispered, ushering them through.

Simon's room was pitch black. Bastian fumbled for the light switch, his hand scraping the wall, but stopped when he heard Odette's voice.

"Keep the lights off," she whispered. She sounded so different in the dark.

From the sound of her voice, Bastian knew Odette was standing in the corner of the room. Callum still stood next to him. And behind them, Simon was rummaging with something near the floor.

"What's happe—" But Callum was interrupted when a blinding beam of light exploded only two feet from them.

Bastian recoiled, clamping a hand to his eyes, blood roaring in his ears. His head spun, unable to form a coherent thought to explain the sudden onslaught of confusion.

"Sorry," Simon said in a soft-spoken voice. "Didn't realize I had it pointed at you."

When Bastian opened his eyes again, the room was lit by a heavy flashlight that Simon held in one hand. The office was almost exactly the same as the last time the four of them had been there. A quick glance around the room told Bastian of two differences. Since earlier that evening, when he had brought Simon the piece of paper, Simon had covered the small window above his desk in layers of black cardstock. All earthly glow from outside failed to seep in, and Bastian was almost sure no one beyond the walls of the building would be able to see the glare from Simon's flashlight. The other difference was the picture on Simon's desk. What had once been a random assortment of torn pieces of paper was now a complete drawing.

Callum rubbed at his eyes, wincing when he opened them. "Will somebody please tell me what's going on?"

To Bastian's surprise, Odette was the one to answer. "It's complete," she said, pointing to the drawing.

Callum raised his eyebrows and joined Simon at the table. As the two pored over the document, Bastian looked Odette in the eyes. She seemed older than she had been that morning. Her permanent smile was gone. The lifted corners of her eyes slanted downward. And her freckles and hair, which had always seemed so fiery and lively, were now darker, almost light brown.

"What?" she asked him.

"I'm just making sure you're okay," he said, unsure what to do with his hands. The last time he'd been this close to her, he'd held her. Was he expected to do that now? Did she want him to touch her?

"I'm fine," she said, brushing past him to join the others at the table.

"Bastian," Simon said, his voice slicing through the storm of negative feelings. "Come look at this."

016:

At this point, Bastian had looked at the drawing so many times that he could probably recreate it all from memory. At the top, many mountains exploding with fire and ash all over a blue-and-green planet. Just below that, formed out of an assortment of unrelated things, was the number 9.81. Planets, stars, and faraway galaxies made up the rest of the drawing, surrounding a massive wheel with dozens of spokes jutting from it. Now, though, the sketch didn't end there—it continued with the new piece Bastian had found earlier.

The drawing was crude, but detailed enough that it wasn't hard to understand. Inked in blue, a dead man lay flat on a table below a window. Two other people dressed in full-body suits and towering helmets that covered their faces stood at the dead man's feet. Outside the window, robotic arms—like the ones Bastian had seen in some of the Arcade games—protruded from the ceiling. Hanging from the arms were naked men and women. They were, without a doubt, dead.

"What is this?" Bastian whispered. The drawing was

so gruesome, so unsettling, that he'd entirely forgotten about his strained encounter with Odette. That seemed so minor now.

"I have no idea," Simon said, "but I intend to find out."

"And how do you plan to do that?" Callum asked.

"You asked earlier what's going on," Simon said. "Well, to be honest, you probably don't want to know." He shifted the flashlight so the beam no longer focused on the drawing, but instead the wall. Light bounced off, and even though Bastian's eyes had yet to adjust to the darkness, it illuminated enough details that he was no longer entirely blinded.

"I don't speak for them," Bastian said, pointing to Callum and Odette, "but I'm really curious why you made us sneak here in the middle of the night."

Simon glanced at Odette and Callum. They both shared the same look Bastian wore—concerned curiosity.

"All right," Simon said, sighing. "Listen, I think we can all agree at this point that something exists beyond the walls. Someone built this place, someone sends us the food and items we collect when we play the games, someone continues to send us children. When somebody Levels Up and disappears down the Elevator, their vitals go flat, and we never hear from them again. And as if that isn't enough proof, someone's been sending us this." He tapped the drawing lying before them. "There's at least one person on the other side who's trying to send us a message, and clearly they feel the need to do it in secret, which leads me to my main idea. Whatever's on the other side of these walls, I'm not sure it's that great."

Bastian once again thought of his dream and the thought that had come with it. Did the walls trap them inside, or did the walls keep something else out?

"But that doesn't explain why you had us come here

in the middle of the night," Callum said, "and why you were so paranoid about us being followed."

"I'm not certain," Simon said, running a hand through his parted hair, "but I've begun to wonder if someone from outside these walls is here watching us, posing as one of us, ensuring everything goes as smoothly as possible. 55178 runs on efficiency. I find it hard to believe that whomever is delivering us things through the Five Bins isn't in communication with someone in here."

Bastian's mind swirled. He gripped the edge of the desk to ground himself. Immediately, he thought of everybody he was close to: Odette, Callum, Thayer, even Simon. Had Milt been the insider, had Dr. Soren? Or was it Mira, the old lady who had given Odette the *Doctor Bliss* book? Kace and Fenna couldn't be disregarded either. Fenna had raised concern about Simon's conspiracy theories. She'd specifically warned Bastian away from them. Was that why he'd felt strange during their last conversation? Had he sensed in her an unknown danger?

"That's—" Odette began, but Simon stopped her.

"I'm aware that's a massive accusation based on absolutely nothing but conjecture."

"But you're convinced of it?" Bastian asked, meeting Simon's eyes. Up to this point, his relationship with Simon had been very perfunctory. They'd never spent one-on-one time together, and their friendship had never been tested. Yet Bastian fully trusted Simon. He always had. There was an earnestness about him that was too authentic to be faked, and his passion for his conspiracy theories was infectious. So when Simon nodded his head in response to the question, Bastian found, without a doubt, that he fully believed Simon's paranoid theory.

"And what will they do if they find us, h—" Bastian stopped speaking when he heard a sound.

Everyone froze, falling completely silent, their eyes suddenly glued to the door.

Someone was opening the store door. They'd all learned to recognize its sound a long time ago—a slow and broken creak that always went unnoticed during the busy hours of operation.

"Were you expecting anyone?" Odette whispered.

Simon shook his head.

Bastian's palms were sweating, and his heart was thundering in his chest.

"Let's go before they see us," Simon said. He handed Odette the flashlight and then swept the entire drawing up in one masterful swoop, opened a drawer to his desk, and shoved the papers inside. Bastian caught a glimpse of a blue folder in the drawer—something he'd never seen before. Once the drawing was hidden away, Simon tore the black paper off the window, ripped it open, and ushered Callum to leave.

Bastian went to the door and pressed his ear against it.

"Don't worry about it," Simon said. "I'm sure it's someone just looking for more food. It's been happening a lot more lately. I don't want to deal with them right now. Let's just go through the window."

Callum struggled climbing through the window, so Bastian gave him a shove.

Odette went next, stepping onto the desk and swinging her legs through the narrow window first before dropping down on the other side.

As Bastian followed Odette, craning his neck to fit through, Simon grabbed him by the collar and put his lips to Bastian's ear.

"I'm Leveling Up tomorrow. I want you and the other two there when I do it." Then he shoved Bastian

through the window and slid the window shut, leaving
him stunned and shocked, already weighed down by the
idea of losing another friend.

017:

They sneaked through 55178 in utter silence. A few lights remained on in windows, but the town was so quiet and so vacant that Bastian would have thought it was uninhabited otherwise. The three of them regularly checked if they were being followed, but never once did they spot movement or shifting shadows.

Everything was almost unrecognizable in the dark. The concrete buildings looked like black fangs extending from the earth. The walls surrounding them blended in with the darkness of space. The moon, in all its glory, cast a low light that bounced off rooftops and sidewalks.

Eventually, they emerged from the alleys, joined pace on the sidewalks, and came upon a fork in the road. They stopped here. Odette looked left where her townhome was, and Callum looked right where his and Bastian's house resided at the end of the street.

"I need to tell you guys something," Bastian said, keeping his voice at a whisper. "Before I climbed out the window, Simon told me he's planning on Leveling Up in the morning, and he wants us there."

Callum groaned, and Odette's face went white. Bastian hated the way the words tasted in his mouth. If Simon managed to follow through with his plan, then he would be short another friend in less than a full day.

"Why?" Odette asked, struggling to find more words to her question.

"He must think he can find more answers down there—wherever the Elevator takes him." Bastian pointed at the ground, and everyone's gaze fell there.

"I'll be there," Odette said.

"I'll be at his door first thing in the morning," Callum said, clenching his fists. "I'm gonna talk him out of this. He can't just bail on us because he wants answers to questions he's not even sure are the right ones to ask."

"It's his decision," Odette said.

Callum jerked forward, head held high, arms trembling at his sides. "It shouldn't be."

"But it is," she said, frowning.

"Just like it was your decision to win the spawning?!" Callum asked, spittle flying from his lips, his face growing redder and redder. "Just like it was all of our decisions to come here when we were kids?! Just like we can't save food for more than twenty-four hours before it goes bad, and we have to wait for the gamers to collect us things we need in order to survive?!"

Bastian stepped forward, placing his hand against Callum's chest while Odette stepped back, her mouth agape in shocked confusion.

"That wasn't my choice," Odette whispered, tears brimming in her shimmering blue eyes. "Those aren't anyone's choices. We—we . . ." But the words were lost in her throat.

"That's what I mean," Callum said, falling from his threatening height and standing once again on the balls of his feet. "Simon shouldn't even have to consider making this decision. You should have had a say in the spawning." He paused, relaxing his fists and taking a long, deep breath. "We're all pawns, don't you see it? No matter what we say to ourselves, we have no choice, no say in any part of our lives. We're prisoners."

Callum turned and began walking down the street leading to his and Bastian's home. His gawky, toned figure looked nearly invisible in his baggy shirt and jeans. Before he was out of earshot, he looked over his shoulder and met Odette's eyes.

"I'm sorry," he said. "I'm just angry."

Then he left.

Odette sniffled, wiping at her eyes. Bastian refrained from asking if she was okay. He didn't want a repeat of her last answer. Instead, he gestured down the road she'd take home. "Can I walk you?"

Still sniffling, she nodded her head.

They ambled, enjoying the cold air. Bastian's nose was beginning to run, but he didn't mind. They were usually blasted with heat, so the cool weather was a welcome change.

"I'm sorry, Bastian," Odette said. Without warning, she reached out and grabbed his hand.

A warm, exciting feeling torpedoed through his stomach. He turned his head, hiding his surprised, blushing face from her.

Realizing that his cheeks were already red from the cold, he nodded and met her eyes. His stomach clenched in an unfamiliar ache at the sight of her face. She was impeccable under the moonlight. Her cheeks, rosy from the chill, only brought out a lighter blue in her eyes. She smiled at him, and he nearly let go of her hand, overwhelmed by the relentlessly giddy feeling in his gut.

"It's okay," he mumbled, shivering from everything but the cold. "I know you're stressed."

"It's not okay," she responded, halting in front of her townhome. Bastian was surprised and annoyed they'd already arrived. Had they really been walking that long, or had he misremembered how long it took to get to her place?

"This is my life now. I'm Dr. Odette, and I need to get used to that."

Bastian barely registered her words. He was hyper-focused on his palm still wrapped in hers. It was slowly beginning to sweat, and he wondered what she thought. Was she disgusted? Had she noticed yet? Was this normal?

"Can I try something?" she asked.

He nodded, too distracted to form a coherent word.

She leaned forward, closing her eyes. His heart pummeled the inside of his chest, nearly exploding with every pump of blood. His stomach spun in circles, and he feared he was going to barf.

Odette closed her mouth, pursing her lips out in the shape of a heart. He almost stepped back, glancing desperately around the vacant street, terrified of what was about to happen but ecstatic at the same time.

He leaned forward. She smelled faintly of fresh fruit, one of the rare luxuries Simon occasionally managed to snag. And he was suddenly aware of himself in ways he never had been before. How did he smell? Had he showered that morning? Were his clothes clean and presentable? How was his breath? Did it reek, or was it okay?

And then, in a split second, the words left his mouth before he had a chance to stop them.

"I think I want to wait," he whispered, his breath frosty and visible in the air.

Odette opened her eyes, pausing with her head still

tilted toward his. "Can I ask why?" she asked, her lips curling into a displeased frown.

"You said it yourself—you're really confused today. I don't want to take advantage of that. I want to do this when you want to do it on a day when your head is clear. Not now." He was surprised at how mature he sounded. He thought for sure the words would have come out jumbled and offensive, but they sounded just the opposite, well-articulated and thoughtful.

For a moment, Odette remained still, and then she smiled, her eyebrows pulled together.

"Thank you," she said. "That's . . . thank you."

Bastian let go of her hand, his heart still thudding against the inside of his chest, and waited until she was at her front door. She glanced back at him, her eyes lingering on his, and then disappeared inside, shutting the door quietly behind her.

018:

"Bro, wake up before I throw you through the window."

Bastian grumbled, lashing out when someone grabbed his shoulders and shook him violently.

"Dude, I'm serious. You'll be tasting glass in five seconds."

"Fine," Bastian said, grunting as he pushed himself up on his bed and opened his eyes. Callum was leaning over him, eyes bloodshot and hair unkempt. "What is it?"

"Simon is Leveling Up today, don't you remember? I wanna talk to him before he does, try and get some sense through that concrete-thick skull he has." Callum turned on his heel and left the bedroom, shouting, "You have five minutes," before disappearing around the bend in the hallway.

Bastian rubbed his eyes, collecting his thoughts as he tried to fully wake up.

Yesterday had been terrible—everything about it. Except for those few minutes at the end of the night when he walked Odette home. He could still feel her frozen hand gripping his, still smell her hair and her skin. He smiled. Even the thought of Simon Leveling Up couldn't bring him down from this high.

***

Most people in 55178 were still waking when Bastian and Callum left their house and headed for the grocery store. The last pink of the sunrise was fading, and a few residents milled about, ignoring the boys as they passed by.

"What do you plan on saying to him?" Bastian asked as Callum pulled open the glass doors to the grocery store. They stepped inside, surprised to see the rotten food that had spoiled from the day before hadn't been cleaned up.

"I don't know," Callum admitted, running a hand through his hair. "I guess I just wanna know why he's Leveling Up. There has to be something he's not telling us."

Though Bastian said nothing, he agreed with Callum. Truthfully, he was more interested in who'd entered the store before Simon shoved them all out the window. He doubted whoever it was posed a serious threat to Simon. Nobody had committed a violent offense in 55178 in nearly thirty years.

They made their way to the back of the unlit store, guided by the early morning light seeping through the windows. When they reached Simon's office door, neither of them bothered to knock. They opened it and stepped inside.

Simon sat at his desk, poring over the drawing they'd completed the day before. A duffel bag lay at his feet, and it looked like the man hadn't slept at all. His hair was frazzled, and there were dusky bags under his eyes.

"Hey, guys," he said when Bastian shut the door behind them. "I assume you're here to try and talk me out of it."

"Yes," Callum said.

"I need you to understand something first," Simon said. His voice was so stern and blunt that Bastian was slightly taken aback. Simon had always used a calm and friendly voice with them.

"It looks like we've gotten the last drawing," Simon said, keeping his eyes on his moving hands. "The only way to get more answers is to get out of this town. And I know the chances of me returning are nonexistent, but I have to try. I have to see for myself what's going on."

"You won't see us again," Callum said, delivering the words with a blank stare.

"I know," Simon said, standing from the chair and swinging the duffel bag over his shoulder. "But I can't help you in here. The best way I know how to help is to get answers out there."

Callum opened his mouth to protest, but Simon moved past him and left his office.

Taken aback by the abruptness of the conversation, Bastian followed Callum, who in turn was following Simon.

"I don't think you can stop him," Bastian said, jogging to catch up with Callum.

"I know," he said. "But I still have to try."

When they emerged from the grocery store a few yards behind Simon, the heat had already begun to scorch 55178. Ahead, a few gamers ascended the steps to the Arcade, and Simon followed after them, still hauling the duffel bag.

Bastian and Callum broke into a run. The heat was so intense that Bastian already felt the sunburn settling in on the back of his neck. Once they reached the steps, they passed a few citizens who cast them odd looks. It was rare to see someone running in 55178. There was never anywhere urgent to be.

Callum reached the Arcade's doors first and threw them open. Even from a distance, Bastian could feel the cool, artificial air. It made the sweat on his arms cold, and he shivered, suddenly desiring for the first time in his life to be a gamer so he could spend all day in this temperature-controlled building.

Bastian stepped through the doors as they swung shut behind him. He stood next to Callum. The Arcade was bustling with quiet activity. Nearly every console was occupied, their marquees lit by an electronic glow. *Water Bliss, Blissful Lumberjack, Blissful Apparel, Butcher Bliss*. Dozens of games, dozens of gamers sweating over arcade consoles.

Doctor Bliss was empty. Odette had not yet arrived.

Simon sat down at his game, and with swift expertise, slipped the rubber cap on his head, donned his gloves, and began playing *Blissful Grocer* for the final time.

019:

Bastian and Callum watched in confused awe.

They'd seen Simon play his game many times before. Roughly a year ago, the food delivered through the Five Bins came already rotted. All of it was inedible. So even though he'd already spent half the day collecting food, Simon had returned to *Blissful Grocer* and gathered the entire delivery of food again. A task that usually took at least four hours had taken him less than one.

So Bastian had seen the man work fast before. As a hobby, Thayer kept a log of all the records broken in the games, and Simon held the majority of them. But Bastian had never seen Simon work as fast as he did that day.

Blissful Grocer was similar to *Water Bliss* in that Simon controlled an avatar who had to avoid threats to get what he wanted. This game took place inside of a grocery store. It was designed as a maze that changed every day, so it was impossible to memorize the layout. Dead people—the game referred to them as zombies—roamed the aisles, and Simon had to set traps or lure the zombies away from the food he needed. If he was caught even once, it was game over.

Simon's hands flew over the control panel, constantly wiggling the joystick and tapping the buttons at such a speed that it nearly made Bastian's head spin. In the top left corner of the screen, Simon's XP read 96/100.

Bastian and Callum had only been watching him play for ten minutes when a draft of hot air blasted them. Bastian turned and smiled when he saw Odette entering. She was dressed in pants patched entirely with bright purple fabric. Her hair was pulled back by a strip from an old T-shirt, and the familiar smile and familiar glow had begun returning to her face.

"How long has he been playing?" Odette asked, sidling up between Bastian and Callum. They stood a few feet away from Simon, who was leaning so far forward that his forehead nearly touched the bezel.

"A few minutes," Callum said.

Bastian met Odette's eyes. He refrained from looking at her lips. Their moment together from the night before still sent shivers through his body. He wasn't sure he'd ever get used to the feeling.

"How'd you sleep?" she whispered, nudging him with her shoulder.

"Okay," he lied. "And you?"

"I feel better." Her breath smelled like mint. Bastian leaned forward staring at her; her entire aura was alluring, intoxicating. "Stop," she said suddenly, blushing and giggling.

Bastian turned his head. He'd been looking at her lips.

The hot rush of air returned, and the three of them turned to see who was coming. Bastian was grateful for the distraction; he was pretty sure his cheeks were redder than fire.

Fenna stepped through the door. Her curly red hair was flattened by a bonnet tied at her neck. She held the hands of the two eight-year-olds who'd arrived a couple days prior in place of Milt. Bastian wondered if the ones to replace Dr. Soren were here yet.

"Here it is," Fenna said as she bent down to the kids' level. The boy and the girl stared around the Arcade with open mouths.

Odette left Bastian's side to greet the kids. Callum was still focused on Simon. Fenna stepped up to Bastian, squeezing his arm with the firm but careful grip he remembered so vividly from his childhood.

"Simon swung by very early this morning and told me he thinks he'll Level Up today."

Bastian said nothing. He wasn't entirely sure if he could trust Fenna yet. Besides, she smelled like breakfast food, and he was pretty sure if he opened his mouth, he would drool.

"How do you feel about it?" she asked.

"Sad," he said, and she nodded her head in understanding.

"Living in society requires sacrifices. Doesn't mean we have to like it, but it demands them of us nonetheless." She let go of Bastian's arm. "Thought it'd be good for the kids to see the Arcade and see what happens when somebody Levels Up. As skeptical as I am of Simon, I'll miss the man. Never was somebody so good at that game as he is."

She returned to the children and struck up a conversation with Odette.

"He's at ninety-seven now," Callum said, pointing to the XP at the top of Simon's monitor.

"It might be a long day, man. Might as well get comfortable."

✳✳✳

Nearly an hour into playing, Simon's hands moved faster than the game had time to compute. He began experiencing a slight lag, and the machine had to buffer for a moment in order to keep up with him. It was a sight to behold to watch him play. Even some of the other gamers left their stools to watch Simon. He had so far collected enough food to keep the town fed for three days. People would feast tonight while the food was still good.

"You're sure you wanna go through with this?" Callum asked, sneaking up next to Simon and peering over his shoulder.

Simon flinched at the intrusion, wiped his hands on his black jacket, and then resumed playing.

"Either I go looking for answers, or we all spend the rest of our lives behind these walls."

Bastian looked around, hoping no one was listening to the conversation, but luckily, everybody seemed involved in their own discussions.

"Is that so bad?" Callum asked. "At least you'll be with us, your friends. You Level Up, and we may never see each other again after today."

Even though Bastian agreed with everything Callum was saying and did desperately want Simon to stay, he knew that Callum's repeated arguments would do nothing to convince the gamer to change his mind.

"Callum," Bastian said. "You can't stop him."

A few people in the crowd caught Bastian's words, including Fenna and Odette.

"He's just gonna Level Up, and you're not gonna do anything about it?" Callum asked with clenched teeth. His nostrils flared, and his hands trembled. Bastian had seen this attitude from Callum before. His friend was on the brink of erupting into anger.

"It's his choice," Bastian said.

Callum raised a pointed finger to Bastian. His cheeks were red, and his eyes glimmered with tears. "If you don't do anything, you're just as responsible."

In the corner of Simon's monitor, 99/100 XP flashed. At any moment, he would Level Up.

Something came over Bastian. He wasn't sure if it was what Callum had said, if it was Odette's lingering gaze, if it was the way Simon leaned over the control panel, or if it was a combination of everything starting with Milt's sacrifice and ending with seeing the blinking 99/100 XP on Simon's screen, but a sudden, fiery urge enveloped Bastian. Callum was right. He needed to do something to stop this. How could he stand by and watch one of his best friends willingly walk into an uncertain fate? How could he stand by and watch Simon choose to disappear forever?

He lurched forward, feeling Odette's grasping fingers brush his arm. On the monitor of *Blissful Grocer,* Simon's avatar moved past a zombie and picked up a bag of assorted breads. All he needed to do was interrupt Simon for a split second. Maybe it would convince him to stay for at least one more day.

Still falling in a forward momentum, Bastian knocked Simon's hands away from the control panel. Then to catch himself from falling, Bastian grabbed the joystick to *Blissful Grocer.*

A splitting *boom* shot through his body. A sudden heat surged up his arms, and then all of his limbs went numb at once. He was thrown off his feet, the joystick crackling with electricity, and just as he shouted out in pain, his head smacked the floor, and everything went black.

020:

Bastian woke to a circle of faces staring down at him and the overwhelming scent of burned hair. Odette, Callum, Fenna, the two new kids, Simon, and Thayer all breathed a sigh of relief when he opened his eyes and pushed himself into a sitting position.

"Are you okay?" Odette asked, kneeling and grabbing him by his shoulders.

"I think so," he said. As far as he could tell, everything in his body was functioning properly. His muscles were sore, and his arms were still numb, but he didn't think anything was broken.

"Why did you grab the controls?" Thayer asked. He grabbed Bastian's hands and flipped them over. His palms were blackened, parts of them cracked and bleeding. He winced, grateful that he couldn't feel anything past his elbows.

"I was trying to stop him," Bastian said, casting a sideways glance at Simon. "I didn't want him to Level Up."

Odette was still holding Bastian by the shoulders,

and Callum stood only a few feet away. Fenna, Thayer, and the two children both gave Bastian odd looks, but he ignored them. Of course, it was strange to hear someone criticizing the achievement of Leveling Up. In 55178, it was honorable to do so, and generally considered forbidden to discourage it.

"Did I?" Bastian asked, trying to crane his neck to see the *Blissful Grocer* game.

"No," Callum said. "He reached a hundred just before you intervened."

"Sorry, kid," Simon said. "The Elevator is waiting to take me down right now. I'd like it if you were there when I go."

Odette helped Bastian down the Arcade's steps. The sun was unleashing its full fury, and everyone took a moment to wipe the sweat from their eyebrows. The concrete walls looked drabber than usual. Bastian didn't know if it had something to do with being electrocuted or what, but the world seemed a little bit darker than usual despite the clear skies and the blazing sun.

A crowd had gathered at the Elevator. Most people were alerted to it because of the screeches it made during its ascension, even though many always ignored it. While nobody besides Bastian, Callum, and Odette had attended Dr. Soren's departure from 55178, Simon's crowd would be larger. He was famous amongst the town, as everybody relied on him every day to gather food.

The Elevator, as Simon had said, was waiting. It'd risen from the ground, its doors open, its seat empty. As Simon passed the crowd gathered near the sides of the Elevator, he shook their hands and gave them hugs. Most of the attendees were older aside from Bastian, Callum, and the kids at Fenna's side.

Still supported by Odette, Bastian followed behind

Simon, as did Callum, Fenna, the children, and Thayer. Everything seemed to be happening in slow motion, and Bastian was sure it was a side effect of the electrocution. His arms and hands were beginning to ache as well. Odette would need to play *Doctor Bliss* and treat his burns. How fitting that he would be her first patient. And if he was being honest with himself, he liked the idea of her treating him.

Once at the Elevator, Simon placed his duffel bag near the feet of the chair and then turned around. He seemed so calm, so reserved. Bastian wondered how he did it. While exciting, the unknown was still terrifying. If Bastian were in Simon's shoes, he would be freaking out.

"Well, this is it," Simon said, running a hand through his perfectly parted hair.

"Whatcha doin' with that bag, Simon?" Garol asked, pointing to the duffel.

Simon patted the bag more to scoot it farther under his seat. "Just taking some memories of this place."

"Where does that go?" the eight-year-old boy asked, pointing to the Elevator.

Before Fenna could answer him, Simon spoke up. "We don't know. But after I leave, a couple more kids like you will come back up in my place."

"Friends," the little girl said.

"Friends," Simon said. He looked up at Bastian, Callum, and Odette. There were no tears in his eyes, no sense of a frown bordering his lips, no fear in his voice. He was clearly confident in his decision.

"Thank you, you three, for your friendships." He stepped forward and wrapped them in a group hug. He smelled like heat and sweat and tin. For a moment, Bastian was transported to Simon's office, watching the man pore over the drawing, discussing the possibilities of what it could mean and what could be beyond the walls. Then, when Simon pulled away, Bastian was brought back to the present, to the scorch of the blinding sun, to the gray of 55178, to the sight of the Elevator, its doors open like a giant maw, the tunnel below it a long throat to nowhere and nothing.

Odette cried, and even Callum teared up, but Simon's confidence must have rubbed off on Bastian. He no longer felt scared for his friend, just sad at his looming absence.

"Hopefully, I'll see you all again one day," Simon said. He stepped into the Elevator, sat down, buckled the five-point harness, and then took a deep breath.

Slowly, the Elevator doors closed until only a sliver of Simon's face remained, and then nothing at all.

The Elevator lurched and screeched, its awful mechanical sounds interrupting a bittersweet goodbye. Then it disappeared back into the ground, and for the first time in many, many years, 55178 was left without a *Blissful Grocer* gamer.

021:

"I think we need to go back to the Arcade," Bastian said once the Elevator containing Simon had disappeared underground.

"Why?" Odette asked.

"My hands are really starting to hurt and, uh, you're the only one who can help me."

Odette nearly collapsed. She held herself up using Bastian's shoulders, stuttering as she tried forming a coherent sentence.

"You've got this," Callum said, even though she probably didn't hear him.

"Let's get moving," Thayer said, waddling over to them and placing his hand on Odette's back. "I'll guide you through the game as you play it. I promise it's not as difficult as you might think."

He began leading Odette toward the Arcade's steps, and she continued to mutter. The crowd who'd gathered to watch Simon leave dispersed, including Fenna and the children. And then it was just Bastian and Callum left.

"I'm sorry," Callum said, wiping the sweat from his

neck. "What I said back at the Arcade—I didn't mean for you to get hurt."

Bastian shrugged, glancing once again at his injured hands. The numbness was fading fast, and the pain was escalating.

"It's okay, Callum. You were—"

In an instant, an overwhelming pain powered through him, and for the second time in one day, everything went dark.

Bastian only heard snippets of conversation during his unconsciousness. Most of the voices were tense, stressed, rising and falling in volume as the speakers shouted and whispered. He never saw anything, never dreamt any-thing, but he was almost glad for that. Darkness was far more comforting than the pain he knew he'd feel when he woke.

At one point, he heard what was very clearly Odette's voice rattling on at a shrill volume. "I can't do it! I can't do it! Just do it for me!"

And then Thayer spoke in his deep, comforting voice that worked perfectly for telling stories around a night-time fire. "You're doing great, Odette. You're doing won-derful. Just breathe. We'll get through this together."

Callum stayed by Bastian's side the entire time. He never spoke, never touched, but over the years, Bastian had learned to recognize his best friend's presence, and he undoubtedly felt it through the whole ordeal.

Near the end, when the beeping and humming of the Arcade finally broke through his unconsciousness, Bas-tian became aware that something was wrong with him. He remembered searing pain—a pain so intense, it had literally knocked him off his feet—but now that pain was gone. Why couldn't he see? Why couldn't he move? Why couldn't he speak?

An absurd thought crossed his mind, and he did his best not to entertain it, even though he failed. What if he had died? Was this death? Was this what waited for every human being when they died? A confusing blackness void of almost all sensations?

Then a voice swam through the chaos. It was musical, magical, and it calmed his horrifying imagination. How long it took the voice to travel from his ears to his brain was beyond him, but at least it was there, and at least it was comforting.

"Bastian," the voice said. "Wake up."

He jerked awake.

The world flooded him all at once. Light pierced his eyes, temporarily blinding him. The scent of sweat and Odette's minty breath assaulted his nose. A dull throb emanated from his hands.

"Bastian."

The world around him came into focus, and he found himself staring into Odette's crystal-blue eyes. His heart warmed at the sight of her, and he felt he could drift safely into a sleep where he could dream and rest and eventually wake to a world where his hands no longer ached and the insanity of 55178 made sense.

"Wake up," she repeated, leaning so close to him that it was nearly a kiss.

"I'm awake," he said. "Unfortunately."

His words earned a few chuckles. While Odette was leaning over him, Callum and Thayer were sitting at his sides. They were in Thayer's office. His door remained open. The beeping, chiming, and trilling of the machines echoed into the room. The three of them looked exhausted. Sweat stains, bloodshot eyes, and frazzled hair testified to the mess they'd gone through.

"You suffered what we call third-degree burns on your

hands," Odette said, pointing to the gauze and bandages wrapping his palms. She held the medical textbook under her arm. "After the electrocution, your body entered a state of shock, and once that shock wore off a bit, you had an intense reaction to the pain."

"Look at you," Callum said, pointing to Odette, "talking in doctor language. You've already changed so much."

"So what's gonna happen to me?" Bastian asked. A part of him wanted to peel back the bandaging and see what his hands looked like, but his instinct for self-preservation far overpowered that urge.

"I'm going to keep a close eye on you and make sure you're healing properly. I'll be changing your bandages regularly, and you'll be staying on this for a couple of days." She tapped a metal post next to him. A clear bag full of a thick liquid hung from a hook at the top of the post, and a clear tube extended from the bag all the way to Bastian's arm.

"Intravenous therapy," Odette explained. "It's constantly pumping medicine into your system, keeping you hydrated and healthy." She smiled at him, and despite her overall tired demeanor, he decided then that she was the most beautiful thing he'd ever seen.

"Wow," Bastian said, truly at a loss for words.

"We're very proud of you, Odette," Thayer said. "You did an incredible job." He huffed as he stood up. "Need to go check Simon's vitals." He scratched his bearded chin. "It's been ten hours, so hopefully, they've flatlined. Wouldn't want every resident of 55178 to go without food for a day, would we?"

022:

"I need some air," Bastian said.

"No way," Callum said. "I made a distinct promise to the old lady that I wouldn't let you leave."

Bastian was lying in a surprisingly comfortable bed in what Odette called the doctor's office. He'd never heard of it before—never had a clue it existed—but apparently, it was where sick or injured people went when they needed a little more care. The room itself was significantly cleaner than almost anywhere else in 55178. The walls were painted beige. Pictures and diagrams of the human body hung from nails. A plastic skeleton loomed over the room in one corner, as if it were personally guarding them against death. And the whole room was lit by a harsh electrical light that gave everything an ethereal glow.

Callum sat on a chair next to Bastian's bed, engrossed in the drawing Simon had left them. They'd been staring at it for a while, but no new revelations had come to them.

Odette had spent the night with Bastian and Callum in the doctor's office, but had left in the early morning to practice playing *Doctor Bliss*. It'd been nearly three hours since she'd left, and Bastian knew that lunch was fast approaching.

"I need to get out for just a second," Bastian said. "We could visit Simon's office one last time before it's given to someone else. Check if he left anything behind."

Callum, never the one to turn down a good snooping, perked up at this, but otherwise refused to show an interest.

"Do you think it's healthy for me to be cooped up in one room all day?" Bastian asked. He shook his arm, still punctured by the needle connected to the IV drip. Odette had already changed his bandages once, but he felt another change was due soon. The gauze was nearly soaked through.

"I don't know," Callum said, looking away from the drawing for one second. "I'm not a doctor. All I know is that Odette said to keep you here until she gets back, and last time I checked, she's not back."

"But I'm hungry," Bastian said. "We could at least check if someone has been chosen as the next player for *Blissful Grocer.*"

"That is a good point," Callum said.

"It's probably not good for me if I skip a meal, right?"

"Probably not," Callum agreed, then he slapped his knees. "Well, you've convinced me. Let's go outside—just not for too long. I don't want to get yelled at by the new doctor."

✳✳✳

The heat was nearly unbearable. It was doing its hardest to melt the pavement, and it absolutely berated Bastian's skin. He was grateful that most of his strength had returned and that he didn't need to rely on Callum for support. He dragged the metal pole holding his IV bag, and it rolled with him on four unbalanced wheels.

"You feeling good?" Callum asked.

"Great," Bastian said, ignoring the throb in his hands where he'd been burned. "First Simon's office, then we'll find out who won the spawning for *Blissful Grocer.*"

"What are you hoping to find there?" Callum asked as he led Bastian down the street. They both kept a lookout for every passerby, silently wishing they wouldn't run into Odette or somebody who would rat them out to Odette.

"The night we were there, when we heard someone coming and sneaked out the window, I saw a blue folder in one of Simon's desk drawers."

Callum came to an abrupt stop.

"You mean to tell me," he said, his long, ragged hair bouncing as he dramatically jabbed his finger toward Bastian, "that we are risking the wrath of Odette over a *blue folder?*"

Bastian shrugged. "I'd never seen it before."

"Well, that's the best form of authentication I've ever heard about! Bastian hasn't seen it? Must mean it's valuable."

Bastian chuckled. Even when Callum was genuinely annoyed, he always managed to balance his tone with the right amount of sarcasm, so he never sounded mean. "It might be nothing," Bastian admitted, picking up the pace they'd lost. "But if it isn't, won't you be glad we checked?"

✷✷✷

The door to the grocery store was locked. Callum struggled with the handles, shaking them and trying to rip them open with pure strength. But it wasn't hard to deduce. Somebody had locked the doors to the store. Why? Bastian had no idea.

"Whoever wanted this locked forgot one thing," Callum said, leading Bastian around the corner of the concrete building.

"Hmm?"

"That I'm willing to break windows to get inside."

They rounded the last corner and found themselves at the back of the building. It looked much different in the daylight. The alley was less conspicuous, and the window somehow seemed larger.

"Here, hand me your pole thingy," Callum said, grasping for the wheeling rod that held Bastian's IV bag.

"What? No, don't—"

As fast as lightning, Callum snatched the rod from Bastian's grip, handed him the IV bag, lifted the pole over his head, and leaned back, preparing to smash it through the window.

"Hold *on!*" Bastian shouted. Callum froze, his weapon suspended over his head.

Bastian crossed the short distance to the building, reached up, and slid the window open with a swipe of his hand.

"Oh," Callum said, setting Bastian's pole back down. "Darn. I was looking forward to breaking that thing." Before Bastian could respond, Callum hoisted himself up the wall and through the window.

"It should be in the same drawer he kept the drawing in," Bastian shouted. He replaced his IV bag on its hook and then leaned against the building's wall, listening to Callum rummage around inside, hissing under his breath when something heavy dropped on the ground.

Moments later, Callum climbed out of the window

and dropped to the ground below. He held the blue folder out to Bastian, a smile on his face.

"I peeked inside. There are a couple more drawings, and I think they might explain why Simon wanted to Level Up."

023:

When they arrived at the steps leading to the Arcade's front doors moments later, Bastian realized their plan of action had a significant flaw that both of them had failed to consider. Thayer was probably in his office at the back of the Arcade. To get there, they'd have to walk past every game and every player, and one of those players was Odette.

"You thinking what I'm thinking?" Callum asked, squinting at the building, the blue folder gripped tightly in his hands.

"How are we gonna get past Odette?"

"Yeah," Callum said. "You know, sometimes I wonder what would happen to us if she weren't around? I mean, don't ever tell her I said any of this, but she really carries the brains for all of us, doesn't she?"

"Yeah," Bastian said, sighing deeply. "She does." The mere thought of Odette sent a tingling chill up his spine. The memory of them outside her house—of the touching and the holding and the talk of a kiss—was still warm, still intoxicating. He hadn't told Callum any of it, nor would he for some time. For now, it was just between him and Odette, their own secret, their own promise of a more exciting future.

He glanced at his wrapped hands again. While the pain was uncomfortable, he couldn't help but almost be grateful it had happened. Because of this injury, Odette had overcome her fears about *Doctor Bliss,* and in some demented way, the two of them had been forced closer together. He hoped tonight, after Odette was done playing the game and Callum left for home, that she would come to stay with him in the doctor's office. That they would get to spend quality time with each other.

"Hey, you kids!"

The voice shattered Bastian's daydreams of Odette, and he almost stumbled as he refocused on his surroundings.

"What's up?" Callum shouted back.

A lanky man approached them from across the street. His face was gaunt, with sunken cheekbones and eye sockets, his skin an unusual tint of yellow. He hobbled toward them, his clothes far too baggy for a man of his height. He was definitely sick. With what, Bastian had no idea.

"Sorry to bother you," the man said. As he drew closer, Bastian realized he was probably no more than thirty years old.

"Not at all," Callum said. "I'm bored and"—he pointed at Bastian—"he's regrowing his hands. What's going on?"

"You two stock the shelves in the grocery store, right?"

"Sure do," Callum said, pulling his hair away from his eyes.

"Do y'know when the food's coming through? It's

usually here by noon, but it's nearly two, and I haven't seen any food come through the Bins."

Bastian felt sweat trickle down his spine. "No food's come through?" he asked, suspicion sprouting in the back of his mind.

"None. I know Mr. Simon Leveled Up yesterday, so that might have something to do with the delay. But I poked my head inside the Arcade about an hour ago, and I didn't see anybody sitting at *Blissful Grocer*. Was wondering if you two have a clue as to what's going on?"

"Honestly," Callum said, speaking as Bastian's mind whirred, "we've been holed up at the doctor's office ever since yesterday. We're as in the dark as you are."

Bastian couldn't stop his mind from spinning. He knew it was pointless to theorize over the reason this man claimed he'd seen nobody playing *Blissful Grocer*, yet he couldn't help but wonder what the reason was. Had the person who'd won the spawning refused to play the game? Was there a technical difficulty with the machine? Or had Thayer simply not held a spawning yet?

"I'm sure, though," Callum said, his sarcastic tone morphing into something more reassuring, "that everything will be fine. It'll probably all be back to normal in a couple of hours." He smiled, teeth gleaming.

"I sure hope so," the man said as he turned and meandered back to the Five Bins.

Once the man was out of earshot, Callum spun on Bastian, eyes wide and hands still holding the blue folder above his head. "So, uh, I guess I better go check on what the heck is going on. See what happens? We leave for *one day,* and suddenly the town is entirely out of food."

"Odette might see you," Bastian added, ignoring Callum's joke.

"Ah, who cares? She's so old, I doubt her eyesight is good enough anyway."

He left, and Bastian sat down in the dirt, situating himself until he was comfortable. The day was still raging hot, and he was entirely soaked in sweat, which wasn't anything new.

If he was honest with himself, it was bothersome how easily Callum could brush off concerns with humor. Bastian had always struggled with that. Anything even remotely stressful or concerning weighed on his mind until it was resolved. Maybe that's why they were friends. Maybe Bastian needed Callum because the two evened each other out.

He tried thinking of a joke to take his mind off the one million insane things going on, but his efforts were futile. It was useless. He couldn't even distract himself from the issues long enough to find humor in them.

For months and months, they'd been finding pieces to a strange drawing, which, when assembled, was the most bizarre thing Bastian had ever seen. It was either history, a warning, or complete nonsense. Then Odette had won the spawning, Simon had Leveled Up, and Bastian had nearly killed himself by simply touching a joystick. Now, he and Callum had a blue folder containing even more hidden messages, and 55178 was without food for some unknown reason.

Even in the glaring sunlight, Bastian recognized Callum's toned form charging down the steps of the Arcade. He ignored the remarks of a few individuals waiting by the Five Bins and bolted across the street. By the time he reached Bastian, he was panting for air.

"So?" Bastian asked.

"Yeah," Callum said, still struggling for breath. "Thayer wants to talk to us."

Bastian cocked his head, a dozen different theories spiraling through his head. "Why?"

"I have no idea," Callum said. "But I'm pretty sure we aren't getting any food today."

024:

Since Bastian's hands were still tender, Callum carried the pole and the IV bag up the steps for him. They entered the Arcade, and Bastian welcomed the blast of cool air. It did nothing to curb his profuse sweating, but at least it made him semi-comfortable.

The Arcade was about as full as usual. Kysee, the new lady, sat at *Water Bliss*. It was only—Bastian paused, realizing he'd lost almost all sense of time since his injury— her third day. She still wasn't as skilled as Milt was even in his last days, but she was clearly getting the hang of it.

Odette was practically glued to the *Doctor Bliss* screen. She looked odd in the rubber cap and gloves, like somebody who'd found clothing accessories far too many sizes too big. On the monitor, her avatar stood beside a body laid out on the table. Several things were wrong with the body, such as a skin lesion, a blister, a bleeding cut, a burn, a rash, and a broken bone. Bastian had seen Dr. Soren play the game a handful of times. The goal was to successfully treat one of the patient's wounds, and if the player did so, the medicine and equipment they used to heal their patient would be sent to the Five Bins. Odette was currently treating the burn, moving her toggle stick in slow circles to make her avatar rub cream on the injury.

Bastian and Callum sneaked past her, trying to avoid her field of vision. She didn't notice them. All her attention was on the game.

They reached the back of the Arcade, and Callum knocked on the door to Thayer's office.

"Come in," Thayer said in a gruff, agitated voice.

They stepped inside, and Callum shut the door behind them. Thayer was sitting at his desk, eyes scanning the multiple screens hanging from the wall above him. His beard was even more unkempt than usual, and he looked entirely spent. Thayer had never appeared to be in excellent health, but this was the worst Bastian had ever seen him. His eyes were bloodshot, dark bags harshly underlining them. He stunk like he hadn't showered in a couple of days. And there were crumbs strewn all along his desk.

"Everything okay, Thayer?" Bastian asked.

"No," he said flatly. He spun in his chair, heaving as he situated himself into a much more comfortable position.

"Care to explain?" Callum asked.

Thayer sighed, and before he started talking, Bastian pointed to the far right screen. "Is that what I think it is?" he asked.

"Unfortunately," Thayer said. He pointed to the same screen. It was a list of vitals—blood pressure, pulse rate, body temperature, ATP, and respiration rate—all of them running higher than everybody else's in 55178. "Those are Simon's vitals. It's been twenty-six hours."

Bastian immediately understood the implication of the situation. It created a vast hole in his gut. He reread the vitals two more times, looking for any inconsistencies or clues, but they seemed entirely normal.

"Last time I heard," Callum said, his face also twisted into a sour expression, "the longest someone's vitals stayed active once they Leveled Up was sixteen hours."

"You're correct," Thayer said, scratching at the curly mess of his sideburns. "No one's vitals have ever lasted this long. Not even in the logs of the person who kept track of vitals before me. This is a record—a very bad record."

"How long do you think we should wait before we really start to worry?" Callum asked.

"We should really start worrying now," Thayer said. "I mean, just us. We shouldn't tell the town about this. If anybody asks, just say we're experiencing technical difficulties that'll be resolved soon."

"His ATP levels are high," Bastian said, reaching up and touching that spot on the screen.

The only concerning thing he could see was Simon's ATP levels: 342.9 mol/L. Bastian thought back to his own. Hadn't it been .10 mol/L?

"I saw that too," Thayer said. "And I have a theory."

He paused, pressing his fingers to his lips. "When you touched Simon's game," Thayer said, pointing at Bastian, "it gave me an idea. One I'm amazed I didn't think of earlier. What if the Arcade games are somehow infusing their players with doses of ATP? The rubber gloves and the rubber cap protect their skin from burning, obviously." He gestured at Bastian's bandaged hands. "But what if the more they play the game, the higher their ATP levels rise? And then when they reach a certain level, say 330.0 mol/L, they Level Up?"

"But what's the point?" Bastian asked. "Your theory

makes sense, but I'm just struggling to understand what the purpose of it all is."

"Me too," Thayer said. "But that's the least of our problems. We better hope Simon's vitals crash soon, or this town is going to starve."

"How long can we go without food?" Callum asked.

"That's something I'd ask your doctor friend," Thayer said, motioning to the door. "Why don't you two go figure that out? I'll keep looking into this, see if there's some way to reset the game or something."

025:

"Bro, you need to talk to her first," Callum said, slapping Bastian's shoulder. "If I do it, she'll hit me. But she'd never hit you, not when you're all sad and injured."

Bastian held up his hands in response. "She's the one taking care of me, idiot. Why do I wanna upset the only person in town who can fix me?"

"You're getting implicated in this either way," Callum argued. "If you make me go, I'll tell her leaving was all your idea. So pick your poison."

Bastian bit his lower lip and leaned against the back of *Sewer Bliss*. "You really are—"

"A moron," Odette said, cutting him off. Bastian and Callum jumped back, startled by her sudden appearance, and then pressed closer together. "Both of you are morons." She glared at Callum, eyebrows flat and lips pursed. "Didn't I tell you to keep him at the office?" she asked. Then she turned to Bastian. "And didn't I tell you that you weren't to leave?"

Neither of them responded. Bastian was gripped in a

giddy, ice-cold fear. Odette rarely got upset with them. It was terrifying.

"You won't heal if you don't give yourself time to," she said, yanking Bastian's pole from him and checking the IV bag. "That might be a new concept to the both of you, but when you're sick or injured, you need *rest*."

"It's a long story," Bastian said.

"Better be a good one."

"We may not want to explain it with other people around," Callum said, eyeing the individuals playing their games.

"Well, you're in luck," Odette said. "I just finished for today. I'll pick up the supplies at the Bins while you two head back to the doctor's office. We can talk there. Sound good?"

Bastian and Callum nodded quickly, ignoring her stern glare.

"By the time I get there," she said, the freckles on her face disappearing in the shadows as she turned, "you'd better be lying down." She pointed at Bastian. "And you better be watching him." She pointed at Callum, her eyebrows furrowed.

"Yes, ma'am," Callum said.

And with that, she left them behind *Sewer Bliss*.

✳✳✳

The doctor's office was such a wonderful reprieve from the noise and the heat of 55178 that Bastian wasn't sure why he'd ever wanted to leave in the first place. It was a relaxing getaway—a rarity in their cramped and public town.

By Odette's request, Bastian lay on the bed. It was a small mattress on a small frame shoved in the corner of the room, but it seemed even more comfortable than the night before. Odette had procured two very comfortable chairs, and that's where she and Callum sat. The whole place smelled like disinfectant, and Bastian welcomed it. When scorched with a ubiquitous, inescapable heat, everything started to smell the same, as if the sun tainted it. This was the one place Bastian had found in 55178 that had its own wholly unique smell.

It was nearly evening once Bastian and Callum had finished filling Odette in on the situation regarding Simon's vitals. She'd listened attentively the entire time, and once they'd asked the question about how long humans could go without food, she pulled her medical book out of a bag she carried now.

"It says here," she said, pointing to a random page Bastian couldn't see from the bed, "that the average person follows the rule of threes. Three minutes without air. Three days without water. And three weeks without food."

"Three weeks seems like an awfully long time," Callum said, echoing Bastian's thoughts.

"Our bodies are mostly water," Odette said, still scanning the book. "I assume that's enough to keep us going for some time. But you're right—twenty-one days is an absurd amount of time to go without food."

A natural silence lulled the conversation to a halt, and Bastian found himself nodding off. An hour or so ago, when Odette had arrived, she'd replaced Bastian's IV bag, explaining she'd slipped something extra into the medicine to help with the pain. He was definitely feeling it now, and grogginess was setting in.

"How long do you think Thayer needs to get it all sorted out?" Odette asked. She tossed her book to the side.

"No idea," Callum said. "At least a few days. I would assume three weeks is plenty of time."

Bastian pressed his head into the pillow, blinking hard, trying to keep his eyes open.

Odette chewed on her fingernail, her face pinched together in a look of concentration. "And the blue folder you found," she said, pointing to where it rested at Callum's feet. "Have you had a chance to look at the drawings yet?"

Bastian closed his eyes for just a moment, relishing the relief it brought.

"Just for a second," Callum said. "Let's wait till Bastian wakes up."

Through his blurry, flickering vision, Bastian saw Callum waving at him, a huge grin plastered across his face.

"I gave him a tad of morphine," Odette explained. "It helps with pain but also makes you a little drowsy." She met Bastian's eyes, too, giving him a small smile.

"It's okay to sleep," she said to him. "Your body needs a lot of that to heal."

Bastian closed his eyes and then fell into a sleep so deep that even dreams couldn't invade his mind.

026:

Bastian woke to something cold pressing against the bare skin of his chest. He opened his eyes, squinting at the bright light a nearby lamp produced. Odette was leaning over him. Here in the shadows, her freckles were gone, her crystal-blue eyes now silver, her auburn hair an almond brown. Two prongs extended from her ears and wrapped her chin. Connected to that was a long tube, which she held the end of underneath his shirt.

"What's that?" he mumbled. His throat was dry, and his lips were sticky.

"Hi there," Odette said, smiling at him and removing her hand from under his shirt. She held a small metal circle. "This is a stethoscope." She took it from around her chin and placed it on the table. "It helps me hear your heart."

"My heart?" he asked, rubbing his eyes. "What does a heart sound like?"

"You wanna try?" she asked, offering him the stethoscope.

"You're sure I can?" He hesitated before he took it from her hands.

"Why wouldn't you be able to? It's mine now. Dr. Odette's."

He smiled and nestled the ends of the prongs into his ears. Everything around him went quiet as if the world were separated from him by a thick wall. He took the small metal disk with his right hand and pressed it against her chest over her shirt. He saw her chuckle, blush, then grab his hand and slid it under her shirt.

His heart skipped when his fingers brushed her bare stomach, and he looked away from her, embarrassed yet thrilled. She pulled his hand up even higher and then forced him to press the disk flat against her chest.

Bastian closed his eyes and concentrated. He had meant to ask about the blue folder when he awoke, but now, with his hand touching hers—so close to her chest, all he could focus on was this moment.

Buh-dum. Buh-dum. Buh-dum.

He'd felt his own heartbeat before, but he'd never heard one. Hers was beating faster than usual. He wondered if it had anything to do with him, how precariously his hand was placed, with how they were alone for the first time since their almost-kiss outside her home.

Bastian removed his hand from under her shirt and unplugged the prongs from his ears. Sounds he hadn't even realized were there before popped into existence.

"What do you think?" she asked.

"Kind of exactly what I expected," he said.

The silence that ensued was not the awkward kind that so often interrupted pleasant conversations. Instead, this one was calming, soothing, natural. He was entirely comfortable in this silence with Odette. It was the first time in days he truly felt at peace.

"You must be tired," he said, noticing her drooping eyelids for the first time.

She gave a slight chuckle and a half-smile, nodding her head.

"Here," Bastian said, seizing the opportunity before he even realized it was there. He scooted against the wall and pulled back the covers, patting the empty spot next to him.

Odette immediately collapsed off her chair and into the bed. Bastian tossed the covers over her, the faint scent of his sweat wafting up his nose. She curled into a ball and then pressed her back against his chest. He was positive she could feel the rapid pounding of his heart, but he paid it no further attention. They were closer than they had ever been.

"Do you still feel overwhelmed?" he whispered to her. "By the *Doctor Bliss* game and all?"

She sighed. "Not really. Not since I had to help you." She reached slowly around herself, grabbed his hand, and pulled it over her side. She rubbed his bandages lightly with her thumb, then touched her fingers to his.

"What is it you want?" Odette asked. "Out of life, I mean."

"To eat. To sleep. To . . . uh . . . survive?"

"No," she said, bringing his hand up to her face. "That's not what I meant. What do you *really* want? What keeps you going each day? What do you think about when you can't sleep?"

He buried his nose in her hair. She still smelled faintly of fruit.

What did he think about when he couldn't sleep? The answer that immediately came to mind was Odette. Especially within the last year, he found that he thought about Odette far more often than he ever used to. Truthfully, there was only one thing that competed for his attention more than Odette, and it was the great mystery of what lay beyond the giant concrete walls.

It was a question as old as time. Nobody had ever successfully scaled the walls or even gotten a glimpse over them. Nobody had any ideas of where the walls had come from or why they were sent here. It was so infuriating, so unknowable, that it had led to mass conflict decades prior. Citizens stopped fulfilling their roles, gamers quit playing their games. The constant public speculation about 55178 and what their purpose was in the world made everyone depressed. Over time, people stopped theorizing, and the topic eventually became taboo.

"I want answers," Bastian whispered into Odette's ear. "I want to know what's out there and why we're here."

"Mm," she mumbled. She felt warm in his arms. Every time she breathed, her arms trembled slightly.

"What do you want?" he asked her.

She took a moment to answer, as if she was considering every word carefully. "I want to know where I got this scar," she said, pointing to the faint line on her neck. "I think I'll be able to understand my whole life before I came to this place if I knew how I got it."

He'd never noticed the faint scar about an inch long on her neck before. It ended at her jawline. "Hmm."

So they both wanted the same thing. Answers.

Bastian had the sudden, overwhelming urge to kiss her then. But for the second time in a week, he fought it, and by the time he decided Odette would probably like it if he kissed her now, she was already asleep, snoring quietly, the most blissful doctor he had ever seen.

027:

When Bastian woke, he thought he was still dreaming. Odette lay next to him in the bed, curled up against his chest, her face nuzzled in his neck. He'd had dreams like this before, so it took him a few moments to remember the previous night.

His stomach churned. He thought this was how it would feel if they ever kissed. Positively nauseating. So exciting that his body's first instinct would be to empty itself out. He took a moment to appreciate the moment, to etch every detail of it into his mind. Her hair was all over the place, thick strands of it coiling in every direction. Her bottom lip was puffed out like a child's would until they lost the baby fat in their cheeks. She breathed at an even pace, her chest rising and falling in rhythmic waves. And that fruity scent about her was dulled by sweat.

Under any other circumstances, Bastian would have never even considered waking her up. He would have happily lay there with her in his arms until she awoke. But his hands were aching, and all the chaos of Simon's vitals and 55178 facing a severe food shortage forced him to act.

He nudged Odette lightly and whispered her name. She smacked her lips, opened one eye a slit, and smiled at him.

"Good morning," she said, pressing her head back into his shoulder. "How are you feeling?"

"My hands hurt a little," he said, stroking her arm with his fingertips.

"All right," she said, yawning. "I'll take care of you in a sec. Where's Callum?"

"What do you mean?" Bastian asked.

"Didn't he wake you?"

"Uh, no. Was he supposed to?"

Odette's head snapped up, and she glanced around the room, eyes wide. "He was supposed to show up early so I could go get some more supplies," she said as she slid out of bed. "It's gotta be—" She glanced at the clock. "He should've been here two hours ago."

"Maybe he forgot," Bastian said, shrugging his shoulders. He sat up in the bed and grabbed the IV bag hanging from the pole. It was empty.

"No, no. I made it abundantly clear when he was supposed to come. He knows that you need constant monitoring. You're his best friend. There's no way he'd forget you." She began rummaging around in a package on the counter across the room, tossing its contents to the side as she dug through it.

"Everything's rotted," she said, showing him an IV bag full of a murky brown liquid.

"Do you think Callum is okay?" Bastian asked. Usually, he wouldn't be worried, but he knew how aggravated people could get when they didn't have their food, and if Simon's vitals still hadn't crashed and Thayer had yet to connect someone to the game, then 55178 was about to go another day without food.

"Probably," Odette said as she pulled her hair back into a ponytail. "You'll just have to come with me to the Arcade. I don't want to leave you alone, especially without a new IV bag." She turned to face him, offering her hand to help him out of bed. "Come on. No time for showers even though we smell like each other. Guess you'll have to live with my scent for the rest of the day."

✳✳✳

They emerged near the grocery store to find the Arcade swarming with people. They surrounded the exterior, clumped together in a giant half-circle. Many of them were shouting, their words blending into utter nonsense. Luckily, nobody was shoving or getting physical yet, but Bastian could identify more than a few who were clearly ready for a fight to break out.

Callum and Thayer stood on the steps, doing their best to answer questions thrown from the crowd. Both of them looked like they'd gotten no sleep, and the frustration was evident on their faces even from this far away. It didn't help that the heat was at its most ferocious. It was scalding. Every surface was at boiling temperatures, and even the shade failed to grant any relief from the sun.

"Now, now, now!" Thayer shouted, cupping his hands over his mouth, so it echoed through the whole crowd. "I know all of you have questions about the food shortage, and I know our answers aren't satisfying. But I can assure you we're doing everything in our power to fix the problem."

"Like what?" somebody from the crowd shouted. His question was followed by cheers of agreement.

Thayer and Callum looked strange, standing next to each other. Thayer was short and round, his legs exposed by shorts covered in stains. His beard, which reached his waist, was so unkempt that it looked like he'd been electrocuted. Callum was almost the exact opposite. He was also short, but toned, all his limbs covered in old clothing, and even though he claimed he was "growing a mustache," his face was as bald as the sole of a foot.

"We cannot connect anyone to a game until the original player's vitals go to zero. Simon's are still reading normally, and there's nothing I can do about that. We spent all night resetting the game, hoping that by doing so, it would disconnect from Simon and we could connect somebody new, but it didn't work.

"We tried unplugging the game and plugging it back in. We took it apart and reassembled it. I even tried manually entering Simon's vitals at all zeroes, but it didn't work. His name and his actual vitals are still connected to that game."

"How do you know it didn't work?" somebody else asked. Again, the crowd cheered.

All this time, Bastian and Odette had slowly crossed the street. They kept their distance from the crowd, but they were close enough to witness everything that was happening.

"I have a system on one of my computers that tells me who is connected to which game," Thayer said. "Simon is still listed as the player for *Blissful Grocer.*"

"Maybe it's a glitch," somebody suggested.

"The probability of the system glitching is astonishingly low," Thayer said.

"But has someone tried playing the game since you reset it?" the same person asked.

Thayer and Callum looked at each other, and Bastian

could tell what the look meant. They hadn't tried playing the game. Why would they after they saw what happened to Bastian? He'd nearly died touching Simon's game.

"We all know what happened to Bastian the other day," Callum said to the crowd. "Some of us saw it. So if anyone is willing to volunteer to test the game, raise your hand."

The once noisy, belligerent crowd fell suspiciously quiet. Everybody looked away from Callum and Thayer, glancing about themselves, searching for an arm extending from the midst of them. But no arm came.

"Anyone?" Callum asked.

Still, no one from the crowd made a move. This time, every member seemed to freeze in place, as if the question literally paralyzed them.

"Well, then," Callum said, "until someone is willing to test the game, none of you can complain about—"

He cut himself off when Bastian raised his bandaged hand.

"What are you doing?" Odette hissed, her face red with anger.

"I'll do it!" Bastian shouted. "I'll test the game."

As if his hands understood what his mouth had just said, a flare of pain shot across both his palms. He grimaced, took a deep breath, and then approached the Arcade.

028 :

The crowd parted for him, and he felt like he was about to receive some great reward or some great punishment. Never had so many eyes been on him at one time. As a child, Fenna had read Bastian many stories about princes being crowned as kings, men being knighted, and criminals being executed. He felt like all of them at once.

He dragged the pole his empty IV bag hung from behind him. Its wheels squeaked, the only noise on the street. When he reached the steps, Callum scrambled down them and lifted the pole for Bastian. The two climbed the steps slowly, and Bastian scratched the back of his neck twice. He hated the feeling of eyes on him.

"What are you *doing*?" Odette hissed. She appeared next to him. "This could *kill you,* Bastian."

"I'm with the old lady on this one," Callum said as they passed Thayer on the steps. "I don't think this is a good idea."

"I owe it to Simon," Bastian said. "Besides, I'll wear the gloves, so I won't get burned again."

"It's not the burns I'm worried about," Odette said,

glancing down at his hands. "It's the shock. If it's powerful enough, it could stop your heart." She grabbed Bastian's wrist, and he nearly made a move to pull away from her, but surprisingly, she didn't try to stop him. She continued walking beside him.

"I'll be fine," Bastian said. "Somebody needs to do this. Clearly, no one else in the town is willing."

"I'll do it," Odette said. They'd reached the top of the steps, and Callum opened the doors to the Arcade. They stepped into the air-conditioned room, his head spinning slightly from the sudden, intense temperature change.

"No. You're the doctor now. The town needs you. And," he continued as Callum opened his mouth to object, "I'd be a coward if I let you do it instead of me."

Odette squeezed his wrist. Her mouth was twisted into a frown like she was about to cry, and even Callum seemed taken aback by Bastian's words. Before either of them could respond, the doors swung open again, and Thayer stepped through, a line of citizens following him.

"I don't know about this," Thayer said as hot air blasted Bastian. "But I'm so desperate, I'll take any volunteer." He motioned over to the *Blissful Grocer* machine, then headed there himself, his sandals smacking the ground with each step.

Bastian followed him as the Arcade continued to fill with people. The last time he had been electrocuted, he'd had far fewer witnesses. Maybe it was a good thing more people were here for this. If it worked, then they'd soon have food, and everyone would be happy. If it didn't, they'd all see what happened to someone who touched a game they weren't connected to. Maybe then they'd understand the solution wasn't so simple.

Bastian sat down on the stool. The marquee for *Blissful Grocer* flickered. He'd nearly failed to realize it, but this was his first time sitting at an Arcade game. The seat was surprisingly comfortable, and the monitor seemed so much bigger from this perspective.

Odette sidled up next to him and quickly removed the needle from his arm, pushing the pole and his empty IV a short distance away. "Good luck," she said, leaning in so her whispering lips touched his ear. "And if something bad happens, I want you to know that—"

"Here you go," Thayer said, interrupting Odette and forcing himself between them. He held out the rubber gloves. Bastian slowly pulled the bandages from his hands. His newly healed palms ached. Odette helped fit the brown rubber gloves over them. They weren't exceptionally comfortable, but he was grateful for the extra padding it provided to his burns. Thayer grabbed the rubber cap rimmed with bulbs and fitted it over Bastian's head, strapping it underneath his chin.

"I'm sorry if this goes poorly," Thayer said to him. The man had clearly gone a few days without a shower. Bastian refrained from pinching his nose closed. "Thank you for volunteering. I owe you one." He patted Bastian on the shoulder, then pointed at the red and blue buttons on the control panel.

"Press those two buttons there, and the game will start up," Thayer said.

"Everybody!" Callum shouted. Bastian twisted his neck to see Callum clearing an ample space behind where he was seated at the game. "If the game shocks him, he will fly back. Make some room."

Bastian looked for Odette, who had stepped away from helping with his gloves, but his view was limited from his position on the stool. He hoped she was nearby, hoped she was watching. But he didn't want to appear desperate, so he focused his attention on *Blissful Grocer,* and once he was sure Callum had cleared enough room, he reached forward and pressed the red and blue buttons.

His heart hammered in his chest, and blood roared in his ears. He was, truthfully, terrified of another electrocution. While he had confidence the rubber gloves would protect him from the brunt of the shock, he knew it would hurt.

The game powered on; the monitor flickered to life. A pixelated title appeared on the screen: *Blissful Grocer.* And below it in smaller letters: *Press the Red Button to Continue.*

Bastian took a deep breath, lifted one finger, and tapped the red button.

The world exploded again. A dull pain shot through Bastian's arm, the rubber cap blew off his head, smashing into the ceiling, and then he was thrown backward into the air. For a moment, he felt like he was floating, suspended eternally above everyone's heads, but then he crashed into the ground, catching himself with his arms.

He bit his lip, refusing to cry out. The fall had hurt worse than the shock, but both were still immensely painful. His heart was beating at a frantic pace, and he struggled to catch his breath.

Odette was by his side in an instant. She was saying something to him, but he couldn't hear her. She pulled out her stethoscope, attaching it to her ears and then sliding the metal disk up his shirt. She listened for a moment, eyes closed, and he did his best not to move. After a few moments, she pulled away and nodded to him, smiling with relief.

Gradually, his hearing returned. At first, he heard only the murmurs and exclamations from the crowd of people staring at him. Then he heard Odette whispering, "You'll be okay. I think you're fine. I think you'll be okay." Whether that was to him or to herself, he had no idea.

He removed the rubber gloves and checked his hands. They looked slightly red but otherwise uninjured.

"Well, that didn't work," he whispered.

Thayer stepped in front of Bastian and Odette, facing the crowd, his hands raised in the air. "A town meeting will be held tonight outside the Arcade. Spread the word. I want everyone here for it."

029:

The rest of the day was relatively uneventful. After Bastian was electrocuted by *Blissful Grocer*, the townspeople quickly filed out of the Arcade. Odette checked the rest of his body for burns or broken bones but found nothing concerning. She sent Bastian to Thayer's office, where Callum watched over him as she played *Doctor Bliss* to gather more medical supplies for him.

Thayer was in and out of his office. He spent the day studying the *Blissful Grocer* machine, looking for any way to bypass its security measures so they could safely hook someone else up to it. When he was absent, Bastian and Callum kept their eyes on Simon's vitals, to make sure nothing was changing, but they were.

Pulse rate: 47 bpm.
Temperature: 96.2°F.
Respiration: 19 breaths per minute.
Blood pressure: 82/59 mmHg.
ATP: 324.7 mol/L.

For reference, they had Callum's vitals pulled up in

a small window next to Simon's. His were similar, aside
from the ATP.

Pulse rate: 66 bpm.
Temperature: 98.4°F.
Respiration: 11 breaths per minute.
Blood pressure: 115/80 mmHg.
ATP: .13 mol/L.

Once Odette finished collecting the necessary items
a few hours after noon, she came into Thayer's office,
changed Bastian's bandages, replaced his IV bag and the
needle in his arm, and checked his heart rate once again.

"You're doing fine," Odette said, smiling at him.
"Somehow, you're doing fine."

"Thank you," Bastian said. Already, the medicine
was doing its job. His bones ached less, and the numbing
pain from the burns on his hands had nearly vanished. He
was in love with whatever medicine she had given him.

They sat around for a few more hours, telling stories
to pass the time, talking to Thayer whenever he made
an appearance, and constantly checking Simon's vitals.
Though he hadn't eaten for over two days, Bastian hadn't
thought about food since his last meal. But now, because
there wasn't much to do, he realized how hungry he was.
His stomach growled; neither Odette nor Callum said
anything. They were probably just as hungry as he was.
At this point, it was better not to acknowledge it.

"I think it's about time," Odette said.

"Town meeting?" Bastian asked. He'd been slipping
in and out of sleep for the previous hour, but Odette's
words woke him up.

"Yeah."

"You know," Callum said, stretching his arms behind
his head, "normally, I wouldn't go. I'm not one for meet-

ings, especially ones that involve a lot of people. But I'd feel bad leaving Thayer out to dry. He's gotta be dreading it."

"Wow," Odette said, smirking. "The little boy is showing some empathy. I think that's the first time it's ever happened."

"Don't act too surprised. You might scare away the shred of empathy I have left."

In obedience to Thayer's request, the street, its alleys, and the steps leading to the Arcade were packed so tightly with so many people that Bastian was surprised the ground hadn't yet collapsed.

From the top of the steps, next to Bastian, Callum, and Odette, Thayer lifted a megaphone to his lips and spoke as he scanned the crowd.

"Thank you for coming tonight," he said, his voice booming to the farthest depths of the crowd. "As I'm sure all of you know by now, the gamer previously linked to *Blissful Grocer* Leveled Up a couple days ago and took the Elevator down. His vitals have not yet zeroed out, but they are in significant decline. But that also means we cannot link anyone new to the game. It has been sixty hours. The previous longest amount of time it took for someone's vitals to zero out was sixteen."

He paused. Bastian watched the crowd closely, looking for anyone who posed a threat, but everybody stood relatively still.

"I have done everything possible to try and override the system, but it cannot be done. Bastian here," he pointed at Bastian, who stood a few feet from him, "volunteered to test the game when we reset it, but the result was violent. I will continue to work my hardest to find a solution to this problem. In the meantime, Odette, the new gamer for *Doctor Bliss,* has some words for you."

Thayer stepped aside and held out the megaphone. The townspeople looked to Odette. She was trembling slightly when she took the megaphone from Thayer, but she spoke with authority. "The average human being can go three weeks without food." These words were like a tremendous toll. It stilled the crowd entirely. A few people started crying, their whimpers echoing up the steps.

"The most important thing we can do right now is stay hydrated. Kysee, our *Water Bliss* gamer, has agreed to work triple time to ensure we stay overstocked. While we can go three weeks without food, we can only go three days without water. So remember to drink."

She stepped back and let out a giant breath. Bastian reached over and grabbed her hand.

"What if we can never play *Blissful Grocer* again?" The voice came from the center of the crowd.

Thayer grabbed the megaphone from Odette and lifted it to his mouth. "I don't know," he said. "For now, all we can do is wait and hope for the best."

030:

Later that night, some of the gamers gathered in the Arcade. Bastian had made room in the center of the floor and set up a circle of chairs. He was there, along with Odette, Kysee from *Water Bliss,* Garol from *Blissful Lumberjack,* Trev from *Blissful Electrician,* and Carlin from *Blissful Apparel.* Most of the gamers weren't there, but that was by design. Bastian and Callum sat on either side of Odette, clearly uncomfortable and out of place.

"What are these two doing here?" Garol asked. He was a burly man with thick biceps and a long, ratty beard.

"I asked them to be here," Thayer said. "And besides, they worked for Simon for years. I figured they were the best representation for *Blissful Grocer* we had."

Shortly after the town meeting, Thayer had gathered the gamers—plus Bastian and Callum—and asked them to meet inside the Arcade. He had yet to reveal why, though Bastian assumed it had to do with the food shortage. Did he have a plan he'd refused to disclose to the public? Was he going to open the floor to discussions to try and devise a plan together?

"I gathered all of you here to help you understand the gravity of the situation. If Simon's vitals don't zero out soon, people will begin dying. The elderly and the children first, and then the rest of us." Thayer paused, allowing a moment for his words to settle in, and then continued. "I have a plan, but it involves all of us working together, and it hinges on a lot of chance."

"You can tell us," Odette encouraged. Bastian reached over and grabbed her hand. She squeezed, avoiding his bandages, and smiled at him.

"At this point, we have three options. One, we can wait and hope Simon's vitals flatten. Two, we can go looking for Simon and figure out what's going on. Or three, we can go looking for food."

At Thayer's suggestions, all the gamers began scanning the circle of faces, searching for an expression that matched theirs. It was like Thayer had suddenly slipped into speaking pure gibberish, and nobody understood him.

"What do you mean go looking for him?" Kysee asked.

"I mean, take the Elevator down and figure out what's going on."

Thayer spoke the words in such a final, deadpan way that nobody argued with him. But Bastian knew he shared everyone else's thoughts about Thayer and his announcement. It was crazy, insane, unthinkable. No part of the plan was reliable. The Elevator only arrived when somebody Leveled Up, or a pair of kids was delivered. And the few people who had tried sneaking into the Elevator to see where it went had never returned.

"That's not much of a plan," Trev said. Like Callum, Trev was thin and toned. Unlike Callum, though, he was nearly forty years old.

"I haven't explained the logistics yet," Thayer said, holding up his hands. "However, as I said before, it's going to take all of us to pull this off, and I don't want to force anyone to do what they don't want to. So if any of you feel uncomfortable helping me break into the Elevator, raise your hands."

Thayer tapped his sandaled feet. One of his toes bled from a dried split. He waited a minute or two—Bastian had lost all sense of time since his injury—and then proceeded with his suggestion.

"Before I gathered you here, I reviewed all of your vitals. The three of you closest to Leveling Up are Trev, Carlin, and Garol. Trev, you're the closest. You're currently sitting at 98 XP. Carlin and Garol, you two are tied at 96 XP."

"What are you saying?" Carlin asked. She was a short woman with tough red hair that stopped at her jawline.

"Well, we need the Elevator to make two trips. Trev, if you Level Up tomorrow, the Elevator will arrive to take you down. I'll hop in instead. Then you'll give me one full day to either figure out what's going on with Simon or find us some food. Then, one of you"—Thayer pointed at Carlin and Garol—"will Level Up, so I can return in the Elevator. If I don't return, wait one more day, then whoever's remaining can Level Up again."

Bastian bit his lip. He'd remained quiet in the meeting so far, mostly because he felt out of place, but even he was critical of Thayer's plan. He raised his hand, the tube from the IV still stuck in his arm.

"Yes, Bastian?" Thayer asked as he scratched his beard.

"I don't want to offend you. My intention isn't to derail your plan, but this idea relies a lot on chance. We're assuming something is wrong with Simon's vitals, not the computer itself. We're assuming you can even find food down there. What if your vitals zero out once you go down, and then we're back at square one?"

"The kid is right," Carlin said. Her gaze was glued to one of her fingernails. "This isn't a very good plan."

Thayer sighed, running his hands through his hair. The dark bags under his eyes were pronounced, and he slumped in his seat, clearly too tired to keep good posture. "I understand this plan has holes," he said. "But it's the only thing I can think of, so if any of you have better ideas, I'm all ears."

As Bastian had suspected, nobody spoke up. It was truly their only option left.

"We could go down one of the Bins," Odette suggested, but before she even finished her sentence, Garol opened his mouth to protest.

"The Bins won't let you through. I've seen someone try. Chopped 'em clean in half. Guts spewed everywhere. Blood soaking the sidewalk."

"So it's settled, then," Thayer said, slapping his knees. "Let's meet here at sunrise tomorrow."

Garol, Trev, Carlin, Thayer, and Callum stood and began filing out the door.

"Do you two need me tonight?" Callum asked, motioning at Bastian's hands.

Odette shook her head. "Nah. Go get some sleep, little kid. It might be a long day tomorrow."

He smiled at her and left, the sway in his steps revealing just how exhausted he truly was.

"Come on," Odette said, tugging Bastian to his feet. "Let's go back to the doctor's office. It's probably time we remove that IV."

031:

Odette removed the needle from Bastian's arm, then poured rubbing alcohol on a cotton swab and wiped the red hole leading to his vein. She fumbled with the bandage but eventually unwrapped it and stuck it to his wound.

"There," she said, smiling at the job she'd done. "You're as good as new."

He shook his hands at her, and she laughed. "Well, almost," she said as she reached for his wrists and began unwrapping his bandages.

Once again, they were in the doctor's office, and once again, Bastian was seated on the bed. Odette leaned over him. Her fruity scent was intoxicating. Up close, he noticed so many more things about her. Her neck was a slight shade lighter than her face, and when she leaned her head back, he could see all the muscles outlined against her skin. She had a freckle on her ear, usually hidden by her hair. At first, when she'd begun taking care of him, he'd felt embarrassed looking at her this way, but he'd grown used to it. Now, it was part of the process.

She changed his bandages, cared for his hands, and he watched her as she did it.

"I know when a man is staring at me, Bastian," Odette said as she moved to his other hand.

"It's kind of hard to look anywhere else right now," he said. She blushed at this, but otherwise ignored his comment.

"Are you scared for tomorrow?" he asked, searching her eyes for any hint of how she felt.

"Of course, I'm scared," she said, tossing the bandages in a nearby trash can. "I'm also starving. In this case, the two go hand in hand."

She grabbed the back of his right hand and lifted it higher into the light. Bastian flinched at the sight of his palm. The blisters had deflated, and now they were white patches of shrunken skin hanging over the fresh pink skin the burns had revealed. A faint odor of blistered skin and medical ointment consumed the room.

Bastian wrinkled his nose.

"Is that normal?" he asked, pointing to the flattened blisters.

"Yes," Odette said. "They popped on their own. It means you're healing." She leaned closer to his hand, inspecting every inch of the injury before moving on to the next one.

Bastian liked having Odette so close to him. For the first time, he worried that she would never be this close again, that the only thing keeping them together was his injury. It made him wonder if he would be willing to stay injured just to be close to her. It wasn't a hard question to answer. He would. For Odette, Bastian was willing to do anything.

"I'll rub some more antiseptic cream on them," Odette said as she peered into the box of supplies she'd gathered earlier that day. "Then I'll wrap your hands again. Hopefully, they'll continue to heal fast. It must be torture for you."

He shook his head, but she didn't see him. Her back was turned.

"I don't know if I've said thank you yet," he said.

She didn't turn to face him when she spoke. "You don't need to, Bastian. I'd do anything for you."

"I know, but I think you've saved my life, Odette. You've made this recovery not only tolerable but also . . ." He met her crystal-blue eyes then. They sparkled under the electric light. "But also the best time of my life."

His stomach dropped. She moved toward him in fluid steps, bent her head down, and stopped an inch from his face. Everything about her was overwhelming—her scent, her breath, her warmth. It made his head spin and his tongue loose.

"You're welcome," she said. She tipped her mouth toward his. He'd never noticed how stark-red her lips were.

He took a shuddering breath, wondering if she wanted him to kiss her. Right now, they balanced a fine line between endearing friendship and exciting, romantic feelings. The last thing he wanted to do was upset that.

She pulled away before he made up his mind.

"Your hands," she said, looking down at them as she gently rubbed the antiseptic ointment on his burns, "are soft."

"Probably has something to do with the burns," he said, attempting to laugh. But she ignored his comment, finished with the ointment, and moved on to wrapping his hands once again.

They spent the rest of the process in silence. Without the constant influx of drugs the IV had provided, the pain began to settle in. However, Bastian didn't complain. He trusted Odette. If she said he no longer needed the IV, then he wouldn't ask for the IV.

Before long, he'd crawled under the covers on the bed, and she sat on her stool, reading her book. Minutes passed, though it felt like an eternity until Bastian scooted against the wall and pulled the covers back. His heart ached, and he missed Odette's closeness.

She looked back at him, her eyes shimmering.

"Sleep with me?" he asked her.

She nodded, then crossed the room and climbed into bed with him.

He curled around her, and her hands found his fingers. Eventually, their breathing found a familiar rhythm, and a while later, to cure the butterflies in his stomach, he buried his face in her hair.

Bastian had no recollection of his home before 55178. Over the years, he'd tried to remember where he'd come from, but the memories were gone, wiped, nonexistent. It wasn't until that moment, with his head shrouded by her wispy red hair, that he realized what he loved so much about her scent.

Odette smelled like home.

He propped himself up on one elbow and then kissed her on the cheek. Her face was so much softer than he thought it'd be.

"I'll kiss you one day," he whispered. "Soon. I promise."

He thought he caught a hint of a smile on her lips, but then he lay back down and fell asleep the moment his head touched the pillow.

032:

Bastian woke to Odette shaking his shoulder. Her eyes were wide. Quick breaths escaped her opened mouth. Her hair, which was always well-groomed, stuck straight up as if she'd been shocked.

"What's wrong?" Bastian mumbled, unable to eradicate the grogginess from his voice.

"I heard something outside. I think something's happening at the Arcade." Odette began sliding off her clothes, a fresh set next to her on the table. Bastian looked away, covering his eyes with his hands.

Maybe one day, he thought, his heart aching in the way it always did for Odette.

"Let's go," Odette said. She'd changed into a fresh set of clothes. These, too, were patched with different fabrics. She grabbed him by the arm and pulled him out of bed. "I think it's serious."

As they stumbled out of the doctor's office, Bastian slipped on his shoes. He was in desperate need of a shower, and he wasn't entirely sure if he would get one soon. Somehow, Odette still smelled wonderful.

The morning air was already warm. The sun had just crested the walls, and the sky was lit with a rare, deep orange. A dozen people jogged down the street, headed in the direction of the Arcade. Bastian tilted his head, listening for any sounds out of the ordinary. When he heard it, he immediately understood Odette's concern. Distant shouting. Not just one person, but an entire crowd.

"Let's run," Bastian said.

They took off down the street. It wasn't common for the citizens of 55178 to run. There were rarely emergencies in the town. But Bastian recognized how slow he was compared to his usual pace. The hunger roared in his stomach, threatening to devour him from the inside. And his hands throbbed with dull jolts of pain.

As they neared the Arcade, the shouting grew louder. It sounded like hundreds of people all yelling over each other, like the uneasy moments just before an outbreak of violence.

Odette's long legs eventually outpaced Bastian, and she disappeared around a bend in the road in front of him. His heart was crashing against his ribs, and his breaths were fighting their way out of his throat. There was no way he could run as fast as she was now.

Eventually, the Arcade came into view. The top half was lit by sunlight, and the bottom half was still the early morning blue of dawn. The sound of chaos was at full volume, and it wasn't hard to spot where it came from. A huge crowd was gathered at the front of the Arcade. They were moving, shoving, their actions growing more and more pronounced by the second. It was moments away from erupting into mob violence.

Bastian found Odette standing a hundred yards from the crowd.

"Do you see Thayer?" she asked.

He searched the crowd for their friend, scanning as many faces as possible, but there were simply too many people. "I can't see him," Bastian said. "But—" He didn't finish his sentence. Odette bolted toward the crowd, and he followed her.

By the time they reached the crowd, it had grown in numbers. Bastian weaved through the mass of bodies, focused on getting past them to the steps. Snippets of conversations flew past his ears.

"Traitors plan to keep—"

"Thayer is Leveling Up!"

"Trying to leave before—"

Someone had leaked Thayer's plan to leave 55178 and find food. Bastian wondered who it could have been. Garol? Carlin? Trev? But none of them seemed like good suspects.

Bastian's thoughts were cut short when he reached the center of the crowd. Thayer stood there, Callum, Garol, Carlin, and Odette by his sides. A dozen people shouted at him, their mouths foaming with saliva.

"If you'll only let me explain!" Thayer shouted, holding his hands out in a desperate plea.

Bastian didn't understand a word of what the crowd screamed back at Thayer. They were delirious with hunger. The madness was evident in their eyes. Bastian would have found this sight horrifying if he weren't full of adrenaline.

"What's going on?" Bastian asked, leaning toward Callum.

"Someone told them about our plan," Callum said. Even though he was close to Bastian's ear, he still had to shout. "They think Thayer is trying to leave the town. They won't listen to reason."

"Where's Trev?"

"Inside," Callum said. "Supposedly, he'll Level Up at any minute."

The crowd surged forward, and the circle around Bastian and his friends tightened. Odette reached out and clung to his arm. Garol and Carlin stepped in front of Thayer.

As if on cue, the Arcade doors flung open. Everyone turned their attention to the top of the steps. Trev stood there, shoulders slumped, eyes bloodshot, hands trembling. Judging by the sight of him, he must have played through the night.

Then the screeching began. The squealing everyone in 55178 recognized. It was high-pitched, obnoxious, nearly deafening from so close.

Next to the Arcade, a gaping hole in the ground opened.

"The Elevator," Thayer said. He moved toward it, but the crowd was faster.

"You CAN'T LEAVE!" someone shouted, and then they swarmed him.

Garol did his best to fight off the crowd, but even he was no match for the mass of bodies. The ones that reached Thayer first yanked on his hair and on his beard, pulling him back into their depths. He shouted, his arms and legs flailing in an attempt to escape, but the crowd was immovable, invincible.

A few flying fists connected with Thayer's face. Bastian cringed at the *crunch* of his nose. Thayer's bloody face appeared in glimpses through the swinging limbs. His eyes were widened with terror, and the blood trailing down his forehead and cheeks was a nauseating sight.

Bastian looked from Thayer to Callum to Odette and then to the Elevator. It had appeared above the ground, and its doors were open like the jaws of a hungry metal beast awaiting its next victim.

He met Callum's eyes, and Callum seemed to understand what Bastian was thinking because he reached out and grabbed Odette by the arms.

"What are you doing?" Odette asked, her voice tinged with shrill anxiety.

Bastian let go of her hand. She looked to him, and when she saw the open Elevator, her mouth twisted into a tortured frown.

"No," she said. "Bastian, please."

Bastian wanted to say something to her, to kiss her, but if he touched her again, he knew he wouldn't have the courage to do what he needed to. He'd do anything for her, and this was part of that anything.

He slid through the crowd, rolling with the shoves, ignoring Odette's screams and the sounds of animalistic violence. He emerged out the other side unscathed. As the sun began its daily routine of beating the town with relentless heat, Bastian ran to the Elevator and leaped inside. He strapped himself to the seat and looked up, watching the crowd condense even tighter. He searched for Odette, scanning desperately for any familiar sight of her, but the doors quickly closed—and then he was alone in complete darkness as the Elevator lurched and began its descent into the unknown.

033:

The Elevator picked up speed the deeper it went. Falling was an odd feeling. Bastian had experienced it only in his dreams, and it was similar to that. He leaned his head back against the seat, tried to control his breathing, and closed his eyes. The moments before he'd stepped into the Elevator had gone by so fast that it was now a blur in his memory. He felt sick about Thayer. Hopefully, the crowd would calm once they realized it was Bastian who had taken the Elevator. Then Odette would have no problem fixing Thayer up. At least, that's what Bastian hoped.

He was, at the moment, doing everything in his power to avoid thinking about where he was headed. Whatever his destination was, it was the place where almost everyone's vitals flatlined. For all he knew, he could be headed toward his death.

He'd already inspected the Elevator, but it was far too dark to make out any details. The seat was surprisingly comfortable, and the straps had locked into place the moment the doors closed. For now, he was stuck in his seat, and to be fair, it wasn't that bad. As long as he didn't let his mind wander beyond the current moment, he was fine.

Soon, he found himself thinking about Simon. The previous few days had moved so quickly, he hadn't had time to properly mourn his friend. Bastian missed him, just like he missed Milt and, oddly enough, Dr. Soren. Would he be reunited with them once the doors opened, or would he find their lifeless bodies?

Bastian chuckled, realizing for the first time how ironic his situation was. Just days earlier, he'd attempted to stop Simon from taking the Elevator down. Bastian had even risked death and burned his hands in an attempt to stop him. And now he was doing that exact same thing. He was literally following in Simon's footsteps.

"Please," he whispered. "Let Simon be all right."

***

Bastian jolted awake. He'd fallen asleep while thinking about the drawings Simon had collected, and he'd dreamed about a giant wheel that rolled over the earth and crushed everything and everyone in its path. He blinked, trying to clear up his darkened vision, quickly remembering that there was no use. The Elevator was pitch black.

Why had he woken up? He was still tired—mainly from the exhaustive pain in his hands—but something had woken him. He remembered it vaguely from his dreams.

When his stomach gurgled, an attempt at alerting him of his hunger, he realized what it was. That falling feeling in his gut was gone. The Elevator had stopped moving.

He frantically reached around his waist, searching for the safety strap releases. They *clicked* at the touch of his thumb, and when he stood up, he heard a slight *hiss*. He felt around, searching for the source of the sound.

A sliver of light appeared before him. It stretched from floor to ceiling and slowly widened. It was unlike any light he had seen before. It was a blazing blue, like someone had taken the blue of twilight and compressed it into a harsh beam.

He peered through the opening Elevator doors into a bizarre room. A track extended out in front of the Elevator and disappeared far ahead when it turned a corner. Platforms were on either side, lined with railings and ladders that climbed the walls. A few doors painted the same blue as the walls were shut tight. Perhaps the oddest thing, though, was another Elevator lying askew on the platform. It was bent slightly, and a dozen wires stuck from the top, their copper cores visible.

Bastian slipped through the opening of the Elevator and jumped onto the platform to his left. Unlike 55178, this wasn't made of dirt or concrete. It was an interwoven metal.

He turned around to look at the Elevator he had been in. It seemed taller in this room, more rectangular. Several spindly arms with wheels attached at the end poked out of the exterior. A long, yellow tube extended above the Elevator.

"That's where I came from," Bastian said out loud, realizing that the tube eventually led back to 55178.

The arms extending from the Elevator reminded Bastian of Simon's pieced-together drawings. In fact, he was pretty sure it looked exactly like something from that drawing. The wheels, he assumed, helped guide the Elevator through the tube.

"What is this place?" Bastian asked. The blue light

made him feel uneasy, like he was in an unnatural place he was never meant to see.

He looked to one of the doors embedded in the wall. Somehow, the possibilities of what was on the other side seemed even crazier than before he'd come down. This cold, dark room was not what he'd expected to walk into. Surely, it was different on the other side of that door.

Then he saw it.

The blood.

It was pooled around the broken Elevator just a few feet from him. It looked fresh, like it had only appeared there moments ago.

And then someone groaned.

034:

Bastian pressed up against the broken Elevator, attempting to flatten himself against its dark exterior. Someone was *here*? He hadn't seen anyone. Had they seen him? Heard him? He hoped not.

The groan came again, and while it didn't sound as threatening as before, he still couldn't relax. He slowly peeked around the corner of the Elevator, searching for whoever was there with him. But the area was just as empty as before. There truly was nobody nearby.

He looked back down at the puddle of blood. A trail of it curled around the side of the wrecked Elevator. Bastian clenched his hands into fists, wincing when his fingers pressed into his burns, and crept around the broken Elevator.

Someone was lying on the ground, blood trickling away from them. Their back was to Bastian, and the blue light created harsh shadows that covered any details about the person. However, it was impossible to miss their injuries. A piece of metal jutted from their right leg, and another one was embedded on the right side of their body just below the ribs.

The person groaned again.

"Hello," Bastian said, not sure what to say in this kind of situation.

The stranger twitched and attempted to look in his direction, but they were either too tired or in too much pain to roll over.

"Who are you?" Bastian asked.

Instead of verbally responding, the person waved Bastian over. He hesitated, unsure whether he should trust this stranger or not. But they were clearly in need of a lot of help. And even if they intended to hurt Bastian, they wouldn't be able to do much because of their injuries.

"Simon," the person croaked.

Bastian's heart stopped. He jumped over the stranger's body, his hands shaking; his skin had become clammy and sweaty. It couldn't be Simon. This wasn't how he'd expected to find him. But when he crouched down to get a better view of the person, his worst fears were proven true.

It was Simon.

His hair, still neatly parted to one side, was matted down with sweat. Bastian could tell the color was drained from his face even in the blue light. His eyes, rimmed with dark bags, fluttered open. When he saw Bastian, he smiled.

"Bastian," he said, his voice dry and raspy.

"Simon," Bastian said. He reached for the metal sticking from Simon's leg, but Simon stopped him.

"No," he said, coughing. "It slows the bleeding. Keep it in."

Bastian was numb. He was confused by his sudden calmness, by how relaxed he was. Beforehand, if he'd found Simon like this, he would have panicked. Now, it seemed like a minor injury. Why that was, he wasn't sure.

"What happened to you, Simon?" Bastian asked. He reached out and grabbed Simon's hand. It was unnaturally cold.

Simon paused between every few words as he told Bastian what had happened. With each breath, his chest heaved higher and higher, like it was threatening to give out on him any moment.

"On the way down, I managed to cut a hole through the side of the Elevator." He pointed to the duffel bag he'd taken on his way down. It was empty. Its contents were strewn next to Simon. An assortment of tools containing a drill and a pickax was among the contents. They were rusted over entirely, bits of them having dissolved long ago.

"I was trying to stop the Elevator by wedging a pickax between one of the wheels and wall of the tube. At first, it was working, but the friction must have heated up too much. The wheel spindle broke off. I didn't see it coming. It got me in the side. And another one broke off and stabbed me." He pointed at his leg. "It was all chaos after that. The whole thing snapped off the track and then rolled out to here."

Bastian looked back at the Elevator he'd come down. He'd always thought of the Elevator as one singular unit, but now he realized there were multiple Elevators. Why? And where did they go?

"How's the town?" Simon asked. He was fighting to keep his eyes open.

"Not great," Bastian said. "Since your vitals haven't zeroed out, we haven't been able to link anyone to *Blissful Grocer*. It's been a few days. We're all starving. Just a little while ago, some morons attacked Thayer, messed him up pretty badly. That's why I came down here, to figure out what's going on."

"Ah," Simon said. "Not so great either, then?"

"Afraid not," Bastian said. He squeezed Simon's hand tighter. It hurt his burned palms, but he didn't care. He was just grateful to be reunited with his friend. It was impossible to ignore the glaring days ahead for him, Simon, and everyone in 55178. They would face challenges, turmoil, and hardship. In Bastian's heart, he knew this was just one quiet moment before a massive, ravenous storm.

035:

"Have you been here this whole time?" Bastian asked, wondering how in the world Simon had survived for so long.

"Yes," Simon said. "Some condensation dripped off of the walls of the tunnel and I drank that. The food in my bag went bad a day later."

Bastian chewed his lip. It was evident to him that Simon was on the brink of death. He'd lost too much blood, and his wounds were too severe. Unless a miracle happened, he would die within a few hours. What did you say to someone in their final hours of living? What were the last conversations people were supposed to have? Bastian couldn't decide, so instead, he just spoke, hoping the company was enough for Simon.

"Have you figured anything else out?" Bastian asked. "I mean, about the world outside ours?"

"No," Simon said. "Can't prove anything. But I do think everybody we send down these Elevators dies shortly after."

"Why do you say that?" Bastian asked, thinking of Dr. Soren, even himself.

"It's the only thing that makes sense," Simon added. "There's no other explanation. We either die, or we're killed, and I didn't make it far enough to find out which it is." He sighed.

"You know, after I burned my hands on your game, Odette took care of me."

"Yeah?" Simon mumbled, smiling softly.

"I really like her, Simon. A lot."

"I know," he said. "Everybody's known for a long time. Glad you finally admitted it to yourself."

The two fell silent again. Simon closed his eyes, his breathing ragged. Bastian thought of Odette, wondered if she was angry at him for leaving or if she was too busy taking care of Thayer to worry about him. He wanted to be with her, wished she were here with him. It felt like an eternity since he'd last seen her, an eternity since the previous night they'd spent together.

"Promise me," Simon said, pulling Bastian away from his thoughts, "that you'll finish what I started. That you'll find out what's really going on here."

Bastian was about to respond, but he was interrupted by the distant sound of a female voice. Every muscle in his body tensed up. His first instincts were to hide or run away, but he wouldn't leave Simon alone. And he was pretty sure if he attempted to move Simon, the man would die in his arms.

"Someone's coming," Simon said, looking down the platform that followed the Elevator track around the corner.

"What can I do?" Bastian asked, looking for any place the two of them could adequately hide. "I could put you inside of my Elevator and close the doors. There's not room for two of us, but I could find somewhere else to hide."

The voices grew slightly louder. Bastian estimated they had two minutes left before they had company.

"Or I can carry you. I don't know if I can lift you, but I can try."

He bent down and began sliding his arms underneath Simon, but Simon reached his hand out and placed it against Bastian's face.

"No, Bastian," he said. "I'm not gonna make it."

"I can find a way to get you back to Odette," Bastian said. Panic was finally starting to set in. "She can heal you. I know she can. She has the textbook."

"No," Simon said, lightly pushing Bastian's arms away. "No, but there is something you can do for me. And I hate to ask it of you, but it needs to be done."

Bastian's chest heaved, and his throat ached. He knew what Simon was about to ask of him, and he hated it, despised it. It filled him with a fury he didn't understand and didn't recognize.

"If the people coming are bad news and they find me here, they might not let me die for a while. They might have questions for me. And 55178 needs food."

"No," Bastian said. His throat was so tight, he was scared he couldn't breathe. The world became blurry as tears plummeted from his eyes. He'd just gotten Simon back. How was this fair?

"They *need* food," Simon said. His eyes opened all the way, revealing an intense ferocity lurking behind them. This was a man who wasn't only confident in his decision to die, but who desperately needed it to happen. "Please. I'd rather die by the hands of a friend than the hands of an enemy. Please do this for me."

The voices drew nearer. It was a man and a woman. They were only a minute away now.

Simon grabbed Bastian's hand and placed it over his mouth. In a muffled voice, he said, "Just press down. Please, Bastian. I'm miserable. I'm as good as dead. You'll be taking away my pain."

Bastian didn't need to consider the ethics of the situation. He knew killing Simon was the right thing to do. He would die soon anyway, and if Bastian didn't kill him now, there was a small chance he could be tortured and kept alive for even longer. Soon, the citizens of 55178 would begin to starve. This was truly the only way to help them.

"I'll tell everyone what you did for them," Bastian said, then he closed his hand around Simon's nose and mouth.

Simon didn't struggle. He kept eye contact with Bastian the entire time until, right toward the end, he twitched twice and stopped breathing altogether.

Bastian pressed his head against Simon's chest, searching for the heartbeat. But it was clear there was none.

Simon had died by Bastian's own hand.

Bastian wept for a moment at the loss of his friend, but then he remembered the voices he heard.

036:

Bastian squeezed Simon by the hand one more time before running back to his Elevator. He struggled to catch his breath. He wanted to scream, to hit something. Rage was building inside of his stomach, and he didn't know what to do with it. He'd never felt this angry before, this betrayed.

He reached the Elevator and, without stepping inside, buckled the safety belts. The moment he did, he pulled his arms out, and the doors began to close.

The strangers' voices were loud enough for discernment, but Bastian refused to wait a moment longer. He needed to hide. And the only place within sight was behind the Elevator he'd used to come. He jumped onto the back of it and gripped two joints where the spindly, wheeled arms connected.

The voices became clearer. They belonged to a man and a woman speaking in low, relaxed tones. Bastian peered around the corner of his Elevator, silently hoping they wouldn't see him.

The two strangers were dressed in identical blue

uniforms. Thick black belts wrapped their waists, and objects hung from them, objects Bastian assumed were weapons—he'd been read stories about them when he was young. Handheld L-shaped devices that fired lethal metal out their end.

When the two noticed Simon's body and broken Elevator, they paused. Neither of them seemed particularly surprised, but neither seemed thrilled or concerned either. To them, this was a mundane event.

"How long has this tube been down?" the woman asked.

The man lifted a translucent, glowing screen and swiped his finger along the surface. "Apparently, almost three days," the man said. He slipped the device into his pocket and then slowly approached Simon's corpse.

"This can't be happening," the woman said as she followed him. "We need more help if they want the system to run perpetually."

Bastian's heart was still racing, and he willed his breath to slow down and steady out. If they stopped talking for one moment, they would most likely hear him. And Bastian somehow knew that he wouldn't live to see another day if they found him.

"It hasn't happened for a few years," the man said. He crouched down next to Simon's body.

"We would've been able to check this out earlier if we were properly staffed. Instead, we waited three days, and now this guy is dead."

"I wonder if we can still harvest him?" the guy suggested.

The woman rolled her eyes and took a deep breath before responding. "You can't harvest someone who's already dead."

The man ignored her. He looked like a supernatural

figure under the striking blue light of the room. "We need somebody in here to clean this up. Looks like he drilled a hole in the side of the pod, derailed it, and then died from injuries."

"Why'd the other pod stop?" she asked.

"Other pod?"

"Back there," she said, pointing at Bastian's Elevator. Bastian flung around, clinging for dear life on the back of the pod. The metal was cool and uncomfortable against his skin. What made it worse was his body odor. Every inch of him stunk.

"Doors are shut," the man said as he approached. "I doubt anyone got out."

"That's not what I asked," the woman said, her voice now overloaded with irritation. "Why did it stop here?"

The man paused, and Bastian risked another glimpse around the Elevator. The man was staring at the strange, handheld screen again. While his whole body was lit by the dark blue of the room, his face was glowing white. "System still thinks the broken Elevator is stuck here. All I have to do is—" He tapped at the screen three times, and then Bastian's Elevator jerked forward on the track. "That one still works."

"I tell you," the woman said, "these elevators are so archaic. We need to find a better way to deliver the people. You should talk to the Boss."

"No way!" the man responded.

Bastian panicked. Every alarm was going off in his body, kicking his flight response into gear. He fought it and instead moved to the right side of the pod. He'd be hidden from the strangers' views this way. All he had to do was hang on.

The Elevator moved much more slowly than Bastian had predicted it would. His toes were pressed against a thin ledge, and his hands were searing with pain. His arms shook, his stomach was clenching while simultaneously drowning in hunger, and he was sweating worse than he usually did in the heat of 55178.

"The Boss will be mad this guy never made it to the juicing process," the woman said. It sounded like they were sorting through Simon's duffel bag. "Where's he from?"

"His pod came from 55178," the man said.

Juicing process? Bastian wondered. *55178? They know?*

A thousand thoughts ran through Bastian's head all at once. They began with the drawing Simon had assembled over time. So much of it made sense now. From what Bastian could gather, the Elevator took someone from 55178 and transferred them down here. Clearly, the guards knew all about this, and they seemed upset not that Simon had died, but *when* he'd died. And if his hunch was correct, this Elevator was heading toward something called the juicing process.

It had to all be connected. The games, the heightened ATP count for gamers, the drawing of mountains with fire and ash and human bodies hanging above a conveyor belt. As far as Bastian knew, these people in the blue uniforms were the first people outside 55178 he had ever seen. And as exciting as it should be, this was the worst situation Bastian could have ever imagined. Simon was dead. He had killed him. And now he was stuck on the side of the Elevator, heading toward something called the juicing process.

He tightened his grip on the Elevator's wheeled legs and prepared himself for the long journey ahead.

037:

Roughly ten minutes passed before Bastian felt comfortable letting go of the Elevator and stepping onto the platform. The strangers' voices had faded awhile before, and he was positive he'd put a comfortable distance between himself and them.

His feet were loud against the metal floor, so he slipped off his shoes and carried them in one hand. While not much about his surroundings had changed, the smell of oil and metal was thick. It wasn't a terrible smell, just strange and overwhelming.

He rested for a moment, allowing his arms and legs to regain their strength. Once he felt strong enough, he got back to his feet, pressed himself against the walls where the shadows were darker, and crept along the platform. He moved faster than his Elevator, which slowly disappeared behind him.

Ignoring his apparent lack of a plan, Bastian instead thought about 55178. Unless the town was in a full-blown battle, someone must have noticed that Simon's vitals had flatlined. Hopefully, Thayer was able to connect someone new to *Blissful Grocer,* and the townspeople were on their way to getting a decent meal.

He didn't envy whoever won the spawning for *Blissful Grocer.* They would be under intense pressure for the next few days. Probably under threat of violence as well. He wondered who it was. Callum, maybe? He hoped not. Callum was not the person to be placed in charge of a serious situation. He loved the kid, but even Callum was aware of his own lack of empathy.

Once the Elevator had long disappeared, and Bastian felt comfortable he was entirely alone, he stumbled upon a door embedded in the wall. He'd almost missed it, walked right past it, but the moment he saw it, he'd made up his mind. He searched for the handle, frustrated to find that there was none. Could it only be opened from the inside? He sighed, leaned against the door, and then stumbled backward as it swung outward.

The room he fell into wasn't lit by the ethereal blue. It was dim like Simon's old office. The walls here were made of concrete, just like 55178, and it smelled cold and wet. Still carrying his shoes, he continued down the thin corridor, flinching every time one of the lightbulbs flickered. Though he couldn't hear anyone, he still walked quietly, as if someone would appear at any second.

The grief of killing Simon was still tormenting Bastian, but it was hidden beneath his emotional layers of curiosity and fear. All of Simon's conspiracy theories, all the ideas Bastian had had about what was beyond the giant concrete walls, all of the strange concepts he'd dreamt, they were coming back to him all at once. He was closer to answers than ever before, closer to answers than anyone in 55178 ever had been. It was exhilarating and terrifying, and his body was unsure how to react. His heart switched between fast and steady beats. Pools of sweat spilled down his body, only to go dry moments later. He was in a flux of ever-changing emotions, and reactions to those emotions. He was even able to forget about his hunger, something that had been gnawing on his stomach for a couple of days.

Eventually, he reached another door at the end of the corridor. This one did have a handle. Cautiously, he opened the door a crack, wincing when the hinges squeaked. Using one eye, he peeked through. He heard voices, but they were distant, and the room he was looking into was vacant and dark. Slowly, he opened the door the rest of the way, peeking his head out in case anyone was watching. Just as he'd expected, he was alone.

The room was circular and huge. The ceiling was at least thirty feet high, and the only light illuminating the area came from down a hallway to his right. These walls were painted, and the floor was carpeted. A few other doors lined the walls, but he ignored them and crossed the room to the open hallway. Here, the voices grew louder. A few feet in, the hallway curved to the right, and Bastian listened for a moment, once again petrified that someone would walk in on him. If they did, would they question why he was there? Would he look out of the ordinary? Would they know immediately who he was? There were too many possibilities, and instead of indulging them, he went down the hallway.

The end of it opened up into the biggest room Bastian had ever seen. While most of the room wasn't visible to him, its scope was still discernable. The metal flooring from the tunnel was here, too, and it stretched out to a railing where a giant, spinning machine whirred away. Colossal concrete pillars reached from unknown depths and supported the ceiling. Ladders outlined their circumference, and Bastian even saw somebody climbing one.

However, the rest of the machine was clouded in steam and fog.

Bastian sneaked to the edge of the hallway and poked his head around the corner. Two men, dressed in the same blue uniforms as the people from the tunnel, stood close together, staring at one of those translucent hand-held screens. They murmured quietly enough that Bastian couldn't hear what they were saying. He leaned closer, risking exposing half of his body to anyone who looked his way.

"Looks like Tona and Jin found a body in the 467 tunnel."

"Did another one fall down the tube?"

"No. Seems like the sucker managed to derail the entire pod. Shame. The Boss will be furious."

Bastian looked to his left when a clear, high-pitched sound sped toward him. It was one of the Elevators—or as the uniformed people called them, "pods." It swerved along a track Bastian had failed to notice was suspended in the air. The two men turned to face it, and it stopped a few feet from where they were standing, swinging slightly until it came to a standstill.

One of the men stepped forward and pressed his hand against the side of the Elevator, activating a pressure switch. The doors opened, releasing a long hiss of pressure. The man with the screen slipped it into one of his pockets and then bent his knees and arms, bracing himself for something.

Once the doors were halfway open, a woman lunged out. Bastian's heart skipped two beats, and the air became trapped in his lungs. He'd mistaken the woman for Odette. She was just as tall, with the same build and the same long, red hair.

She shouted, leaped out of the pod, and immediately

began swinging her arms. The man closest to her had to duck one of her punches. Then, in one swift movement, he straightened his back and swung at the woman's face. His fist connected with her temple, and she collapsed instantly. Her limp body lay crumpled on the floor. The guard who'd been crouched in the defensive position shrugged his shoulders. "You got a lucky punch," he said.

The other guy laughed. "Come on," he said as he bent down and grabbed the woman by her wrists. "Help me lift her. Boss is gonna want to see this one."

038:

Bastian followed them without thinking. One moment, they were hauling the red-haired woman away, and the next, he was following them, sticking to the edges of the giant room, glancing over his shoulder every few seconds to ensure he wasn't being followed. He needed to know who this "Boss" was and what interest he had with this woman. He needed to know much more than that, but at least this was a start.

Luckily for him, this area of the room was empty. The only other person in sight was the man climbing the ladder. But he was so far away and so high up that Bastian wasn't concerned about being seen by him.

The room eventually ended at a wall lined with a dozen numbered doors. The man carrying the unconscious woman's feet used his back to open door number eight. The two of them struggled into what appeared to be another narrow hallway, and then they were gone. Bastian ran to the door, held his breath, and pressed his ear against it. The two men had begun speaking again, and Bastian waited until their voices were so faint that he had to stop breathing in order to hear them. He pushed open the door, shoes still in hand, and crept into the hallway. This one was nicer than the last. The floor was carpeted, the walls were painted, the ceiling had domed lights placed every five feet, and on his left side were windowed rooms, all of which were covered by blinds.

The men were at the other end of the hallway, entering through a door that revealed a room lit only by candle. Once the door had shut with an audible *click,* Bastian began inching his way down the hallway. He peeked through the blinds of each window he passed, grateful to find that not a single room was occupied. He checked the doorknob when he passed the room nearest to the end. It was unlocked. If he needed to hide for any reason, this office would be an option.

Once at the door at the end of the hallway, he leaned as close as possible to the blind-covered window and peered through the tiny visible portion of the closed slats.

The two men stood on either side of a big wooden desk. A huge man sat behind it. His shoulders were broad and imposing, his toned chest was covered by a fitted shirt, and his arms were thicker than most people's thighs. Bastian searched for a good look at the Boss's face, but he couldn't see it.

The men had laid the woman out along the table. She was still unconscious, and her arm was draped over the edge as if reaching for the ground.

"Came from 3376," the man on the left said, his voice muffled by the door.

Bastian clamped a hand over his mouth, his hand pummeled with pain. He needed to hear this. Every piece of him needed to hear this.

"Is she her?" the other man asked.

The question was so sudden and so strange that Bastian logged it away for future reference. So far, it felt like everyone here had been speaking in code. Hopefully, he'd be able to piece it all together soon.

The Boss stood up, and Bastian swore he felt the ground shake. This man was gargantuan, almost comically so.

The men stepped back when the Boss leaned over the woman. He inspected her face for a moment, lingering on her closed eyes. Then he lifted one finger, the size of a joystick from one of the Arcade games, and pulled the woman's face toward him. He brushed her hair aside, revealing more of her cheek and her neck. He spent a moment staring at her, his eyes darting along her skin. He touched her neck, then fell back into his seat, the entire room shaking from his landing.

"No," he announced, his voice louder than the boom of an explosion. "Not her."

The two men quickly grabbed either end of the woman, stepped away from the desk, and turned toward the door.

Bastian stepped away and slipped soundlessly into the room next to him. He shut the door quietly behind him and found himself in a bland and empty space. A couch rested against one wall, a desk on the other. There was a framed picture of a man and a woman hanging above the desk. Aside from that, the office was entirely bare.

He returned his attention to the window, pulled the blinds back slightly with his finger, and watched as the two men carried the woman away.

"What was that?" Bastian whispered to himself. His heart was racing, and his palms were sweating once again.

He was growing frustrated. The puzzle he'd hoped to solve was only growing more and more complex. The solution seemed more out of reach than ever before. The only things he had definitively learned since arriving were that the people seemed to all wear blue uniforms, someone referred to as "the Boss" was in charge, and a woman who looked like Odette had been taken to him.

Oh, and Simon had been lying abandoned in some dark tunnel, slowly bleeding out for three days until Bastian found him and subsequently killed him.

The memory was like a dagger to Bastian's gut, and he doubled over, a sudden urge to vomit making him dizzy. He swallowed the bile, but it did no good. Within seconds, it was gushing from his mouth, burning his esophagus, splashing onto the carpet before his bare feet.

When he thought of how Simon's clammy lips had felt beneath his fingers, how he'd felt his friend twitch moments before his demise, Bastian retched again, backing away, grasping at the air with his free hand. He couldn't get rid of the cyclical memory of his friend dying . . . it would haunt him for the rest of his life.

Thud.

The sound startled Bastian. He wiped the bile from his mouth.

Thud. Thud. Thud.

It was the Boss. He was leaving his office. Bastian ran to the window and peered out the blinds. The Boss stood in the hallway. The only part of his face visible was his chin, and it swiveled back and forth, as if he was debating leaving or staying.

Bastian moved for a better view, but froze when he dropped his shoes.

The sound of them hitting the ground could not have possibly been as loud as he thought it was, but Bastian's ears had never failed him. He pressed himself against the wall, shaking, trembling, his breath begging to be let out in enormous heaves.

The Boss turned his head toward the door Bastian hid behind. One long, beefy arm appeared from his side, reaching for the doorknob.

Bastian's heart slammed in his chest. He was convinced he was petrified, but his own arm was already moving.

The Boss touched the doorknob.

Just as he twisted it, Bastian reached up and locked the door. The doorknob froze. The Boss rattled it two times. He grunted, and then he left down the hallway.

039:

Bastian waited for half an hour in the stench of his own vomit before he garnered the strength to get up and move. He was entirely spent. He'd thrown up what little food was left in his system, his stomach burned, and now his energy was sapped. He'd never been hungrier in his life.

He sat against the wall for what seemed like hours until he gathered the strength to get back to his feet. He slipped his shoes back on, barely recognizing that his hands were in pain. Every other sensation in his body was so much more severe—the hunger, the exhaustion, the bile swirling at the depths of his stomach, the fear of the unknown, and the ache of missing Odette and Callum. Compared to all of that, the pain in his hands was nothing.

He left the room, and a quick glance into the Boss's office proved that the Boss had yet to return. Bastian dragged himself down the hallway and emerged into the same weird area as before. The pillars appeared in spurts through the smog, and when they became visible, Bastian saw no one climbing the ladder.

Sounds of heavy machinery and people's muffled shouts bounced off the concrete walls. Bastian remained aware of his surroundings, but he felt his attention waning. He was tired. The only thing that could cure him now was food and sleep.

Eventually, Bastian found stairs amongst all the doorways. He descended them carefully, convinced that he'd seen someone following him only moments before. He was aware he had no plan, that he was wandering aimlessly in hopes that fate would lead him to wherever he needed to go. The truth was, he had no idea what to do, no place to go, no one to find. He'd already accomplished his first goal, which was to solve the *Blissful Grocer* problem. While a smidgen of doubt—doubt born from fear—remained within him, he was confident that Thayer had connected someone new to the game, that 55178 was back to eating. However, Bastian had mentally moved on to his next goal: solving *the* mystery.

The mystery was a vague description. In truth, it was an amalgamation of previously unanswerable questions and conspiracy theories. Who was sending the children to 55178 and why? What was the purpose behind the Arcade games? What really happened to people when they Leveled Up? What lay beyond (not below) the concrete walls?

The list was endless, and Bastian still had no solid answers.

The stairs took him down many flights. For some reason, his instincts told him the deeper he went, the safer he was. But as he descended, the darkness grew thicker, the damp smell became more pungent, and his eyelids grew heavier. He was sure someone was following him now, a hooded figure wearing a dark robe. But since they hadn't approached him or threatened him, he didn't feel they were a threat.

At the bottom of the stairs, in a recess of blackness, he found a door. The handle was rusty, but his wet bandages protected his hands. He took a deep breath, parts of his body trembling from hunger and exhaustion, and pushed it open.

Light blinded him, and fresh, cool air assaulted his skin. He held his arm in front of his eyes, waiting for them to adjust. Then he took in his surroundings.

He was in a city, one that was far beyond the size of 55178. As far as he could tell, no walls surrounded the city's edges, and the buildings were much bigger and made from materials other than concrete. Some were tall, some were wide, some were made entirely of glass, while others had minimal windows. But it wasn't the buildings or lack of walls that surprised Bastian the most. It was the people.

Thousands and thousands of people bustled about the streets. Some wore clothes Bastian had never seen, like black jackets with folded edges, strings of fabric tied around their necks, and shirts that didn't end until they reached the wearer's ankles. Some wore clothes similar to the ones Bastian did. Regular pants, T-shirts, sweatshirts, and shoes that were splitting in areas. Yet Bastian's fascination didn't stop with their clothes. No, the most incredible thing about them was the color of their hair.

Everyone in 55178 had red hair aside from the elderly, whose hair sometimes faded to a light blond or white. While different shades existed, Bastian had never known anyone to have another color. But standing here on the edge of this street, watching countless people pass by him in multiple directions, he saw all different colors of hair. Brown, black, blond. One woman's hair was even *purple*.

Each person was so uniquely different that Bastian wondered if anybody recognized each other.

Someone grabbed Bastian by his waist and yanked him backward. He screamed, but a hand clamped down hard against his mouth. His heart nearly exploded in his chest as he struggled to break free of this ambush. The door leading to the world outside swung shut on its own.

"Shut up!" someone hissed.

Bastian flailed for a moment longer, desperately hoping he could find the strength to break free.

"Stop moving! I'm not here to hurt you."

Reluctantly, Bastian calmed down. If he was caught, then he was caught, and there was no way around it. But if they weren't here to hurt him, then maybe he had nothing to worry about.

"I'm Maeve," the stranger in the dark said. "You're from 55178, right? You must have gotten my messages. Welcome to Hub City."

040:

Bastian stuttered, struggling for words, but Maeve ignored him. She grabbed him by the collar of his shirt and lifted him to his feet.

"Listen," she said. "Don't take this personal, but you stink."

Before he could protest, she opened the door leading to Hub City and dragged him outside. His instinct was to resist her and dive back into the shadows, but nobody heeded them. The people passing by didn't so much as glance at him. He was, by all intents and purposes, invisible.

"I have questions," he said, finally forcing proper words from his throat. With her hand still on his collar, she dragged him into the crowd of people. She wove them through the mass of bodies, and still, he was surprised that nobody looked at him. Couldn't they tell that he wasn't from here?

"Hold them," she said, "until we get somewhere quiet."

He bit his lip even though questions barraged his

mind. The biggest of them all: Who was Maeve? She'd told him he must have received her messages. The messages in the food? Or had she mistaken him for someone else? How many cities was she sending cryptic notes to? Should he be fighting her off? Was she a dangerous person leading him to a dangerous place?

His worries were quelled when they emerged from the crowd into shadowed alleyways. Here, the breeze was cooler, the air quieter, and the closeness of the buildings was familiar. It was the first time he'd gotten a good look at Maeve's face. She was pretty, with full, round cheeks, rich brown eyes that slanted upward, and thin lips perpetually curled in a smile. He thought her hair was red, but he wasn't entirely sure. It looked too dark.

"Where are we going?" he asked when she came to a stop and faced him. He was out of breath, and his muscles and belly still ached from starvation.

"Somewhere close," she responded, glancing about them.

"How much longer?"

"Not long," she said, turning again.

"Do you have food?" he asked. The question seemed so pathetic when it passed his lips that he wished he could swallow it back.

She eyed him, one eyebrow arched. "Where we're going, yes. Why do you ask?"

"I haven't eaten in about four days," he said. He noticed how his hands shook, how his knees felt like rubber, how his eyelids fought to close in a desire for an escape from the hunger rather than rest.

"Oh my," she said, suddenly realizing just how thin he appeared. "I promise, it's only a few minutes away. I'll make sure you get the dinner of your life."

✳✳✳

Maeve hadn't been lying. It only took them five minutes to reach a series of abandoned buildings. Many were crumbling, chunks missing from their exterior, their bricks scattered upon the ground. Almost no windows were intact, and it appeared people had taken valuable items such as the doors, signs, and pieces of surrounding fences. The ground was mostly packed dirt, with weeds and patches of grass popping up from beneath the ground every few feet.

She took him to a building near the center of the desolated lot. Compared to the structures surrounding it, it was in the best shape by far. They stepped underneath a porch covering supported by two cracked pillars and through a set of double doors. Inside, shelves lined the floor, not unlike the grocery store in 55178, but here they were stacked with books, not food. Old couches and chairs lined the walls, and cobwebs hung from the corners of the ceiling. Though Bastian had never seen one— had never even known they existed before this moment— he assumed this was a bookstore.

"I was expecting less books and more food," Bastian said.

Maeve rolled her eyes but smiled. He would've found some satisfaction in his own joke, but the hunger within him was screaming for attention. He hadn't realized it until that moment, but the edges of his vision were blackening. Fatigue, starvation, pain, and the emotional trauma of killing Simon were finally taking their toll. He knew he was moments away from passing out.

He followed her to the back of the store. There, she opened a door that led into a dark, windowless room. Maeve reached into her pocket and pulled out a flashlight, the beam of which was dull. A metal spiral staircase ascended to the ceiling at the back of the room. She took Bastian by the hand, and together they climbed the stairs.

Bastian was in a hypnotic state. His body was moving on its own, acting because it knew food was close. His mind was nearly gone. He needed sleep, he needed energy, he needed answers.

The stairs dead-ended. Bastian stood next to Maeve on a platform designed to fit only one person. She reached up and slowly pounded her knuckles against the ceiling three times, then gave it five quick raps.

Bastian heard shuffling above, or was it his dreams? He couldn't be sure.

A panel in the ceiling opened, and light spilled through. A rope ladder dropped down to their feet. Maeve handed it to Bastian. He was so tired. He wasn't sure he could climb. But his feet and his sore and spent hands moved anyway. One after the other. Then someone grabbed Bastian by the elbow and pulled him up and over the ledge.

"Need some medical attention," he heard someone say. But their voice was so far away that he must have imagined it.

"We'll take care of you," the same voice said.

And then Bastian slipped into unconsciousness.

041:

When Bastian woke, he thought he was still dreaming of floating amongst the clouds. The buzzing, hard light above him was the sun. The faint throbbing in his hands was his heartbeat, just stronger. Then the groggy veil lifted from his mind, and his eyes were able to discern between his imagination and reality.

He lay in a bed—the softest bed he'd ever touched—in a room like the doctor's office from 55178. For a second, he thought he was there, that the starvation problem in the town had been a nightmare, that everything was still running smoothly. But he knew it was false hope. He was in a place called Hub City, hiding above an abandoned bookstore.

The room was small. It could fit maybe one more patient. Like Odette's office, this one had a desk and a chair. The biggest difference was the cabinets lining the wall. One of them was ajar, and Bastian spotted dozens of vials lining the shelves.

He glanced down at his hands. The bandages had been replaced. They no longer wrapped his hands.

Instead, they seemed to be glued over his burns. Not only that, they felt infinitely better, almost like he'd never been injured in the first place.

"Glad to see you're awake."

Bastian flinched, screamed, and flipped over in the bed.

Maeve sat in a brown chair in the corner behind him. Her arms were folded, and light brown hair fell past her shoulders. Why everyone had differently colored hair here, Bastian still had no idea.

"Was I out for long?"

"Only a couple hours," she said. "They pumped you full of fluids. You were really dehydrated."

"Oh," Bastian said, recognizing the symptoms he felt earlier. "Makes sense."

"You said you had questions earlier," Maeve said. She stood up and dragged the armchair closer to Bastian's bed. "But before I answer any, I have some questions for you."

"Oh?"

"Where are you from?" She leaned forward, her elbows on her knees. She really was a beautiful girl, but something about her demeanor intimidated Bastian. He felt that he would be compelled to answer her questions even if he didn't want to.

"55178," he said.

"And what's your name?"

"Bastian."

"All right," she said, biting at one of her fingernails. "What are your questions?"

He was confused by her sudden shift. She'd made it sound like she planned on asking him intense questions for over an hour, but apparently, she'd only wanted to know two basic things. He shrugged his shoulders, deciding that analyzing her wasn't worth his efforts. "I have tons," he said, taking a deep breath, "but I'll try to ask them one at a time."

Maeve raised an eyebrow at him, and he looked away sheepishly.

"What is this place?"

"Hub City," she said, as if that was meant to answer everything.

"But what's a Hub City?"

"All right, Bastian," she said, leaning back in her chair, "I'm going to explain to you what this place is, how it works, and why you were sent to 55178 at eight years old, but it's going to require you to stretch the limits of your imagination. My explanation will contain concepts you've never been taught, words you may not understand, and answers you definitely won't like. Are you ready for that?"

As far back as Bastian could remember, he'd dreamt about what was beyond the walls. Like most other citizens of 55178, an instinct buried deep in his mind told him that there was more to life than he understood, that sinister answers existed beyond the walls. It was an instinct some, like Simon, embraced, while others, like Fenna, rejected. He'd always fallen somewhere in the middle. So when Maeve asked him if he was ready for all the answers to all the questions of existence, that same instinct begged him to say yes, while another instinct urged him to flee.

With a shaky breath, he said, "Yes."

"Then let's get started," Maeve said.

✳✳✳

"Here in Hub City," Maeve began, staring at the wall across from her, "we're all employed with specific jobs to help run a perpetual machine called Totem. It's very similar to how your town, 55178, and all the others like it function. You're either a gamer or a townsperson who supports the town in some way."

"I stocked shelves," Bastian said, pointing at himself. "With food."

"Exactly," Maeve said, her lips pressing into a harsh line. "What you don't realize is the gamers from your town are also, in a sense, helping to run Totem. You know the gloves they wear, those weird hats they put on their heads when they play?"

Bastian nodded. He knew all too well. His hands were proof of that.

"When they play, the games generate something called infrared light. The infrared light creates an organism in their body called mitochondria. The mitochondria then fuel something called ATP."

"Adenosine triphosphate," Bastian said, remembering back to what Simon had taught them.

"Good job," Maeve said, offering him another smile. "ATP is what gives our bodies energy. If we have too little of it, like you do now, we don't function too well. Funnily enough, if we have too much, nothing really happens. Our bodies can contain massive, massive amounts of ATP.

"When a gamer reaches a threshold of roughly 320 mol/L, they 'Level Up,' and we send the pods to retrieve them."

"Then what happens to them?" Bastian asked.

"Well," Maeve said, her face scrunching up, "that's the part you're *really* not going to like."

042:

Bastian already knew they died—that was confirmed when he found Simon. He shifted in his seat . . . What could be worse than dying?

"The pod brings them from their town down to the factory I found you in. Obviously, you managed to get out of the pod earlier—which I want you to tell me about later—but virtually nobody does. They are then deposited in something called the juicer."

Bastian remembered the two people from the tunnel referring to juicing. What had they said about Simon? That he couldn't be juiced since he was already dead?

"And the juicer . . ." Maeve sighed again. It was clear she was uncomfortable with the explanation, but Bastian said nothing. He needed these answers, no matter how painful they were. "The juicer is a giant machine that melts down the individual and then extracts the ATP from their cells."

Bastian froze.

"What?" he asked, his stomach broiling with another hot, sick feeling.

"You heard me," Maeve said. Her cheeks grew green, and she placed a hand over her stomach as if she, too, were about to be sick.

"You're telling me that everyone in 55178 who Leveled Up was *melted down?*"

She nodded. The first person Bastian thought of was Dr. Soren. She'd been so excited the last time he'd seen her, so thrilled to finally see what happened after she Leveled Up. And then she'd been cooked, melted, and mined for invisible things within her body.

"What about Milt?" he blurted out.

"What? Who?" Maeve tilted her head to the side.

"Milt, he was my friend. He never Leveled Up, so we had to . . . um . . . sacrifice him." Bastian thought back to Milt's final moments, relieved he hadn't been tortured in death. "Why didn't they want his ATP? It was almost there."

"Anything less than a full charge isn't worth extracting." Maeve chewed the inside of her lower lip. "It uses more energy than is garnered from the person."

Bastian opened his mouth, but the words didn't come. He nodded at Maeve.

"Part of the energy extracted from the individual," Maeve continued, clearly deciding it was better to power through the rest of the explanation than get hung up on the juicing aspect, "is used to run the electricity of Hub City and all the other towns like 55178. The rest of it, well seventy percent, is used to power Totem."

Bastian wasn't entirely sure how he was able to move past the idea of juicing, of how all the people he'd known who Leveled Up were boiled into liquid, but his mind was already spinning the new information presented by Maeve. The innate need for answers overpowered the sickening feeling in his gut.

"I'm not sure how much information you had access to, but this is where you might get a little lost. We live on something called a planet, which is essentially an enormous rock floating through existence. We call it Earth."

Bastian had grasped the concept of planets at a young age, but having a proper name for the planet they lived on was somehow comforting.

"Right now, we are in Totem, a giant machine extending from the ground to the sky. We're situated somewhere between the stratosphere and mesosphere." She caught Bastian's confused frown. "Basically two layers of different types of air."

"Ah," he said.

"There are two Totems on Earth. One in the South Pole, on the opposite side of the planet. And this one here in the North Pole. A Totem looks something like this." She produced a folded slip of paper from a pocket in her jacket. She laid it out flat across her thighs. It looked like the beginning of a design for a wheel. The center was labeled Hub City. Roughly four dozen spokes extended from Hub City; they were topped with squares.

"Each of these," she said, pointing at one of the spokes, "is like the one you came down. Long tubes that the pods travel through. The tubes extend to a city like yours. Like 55178."

"What's the purpose of Totem?" Bastian asked. He was unable to contain himself. He needed answers faster than she was delivering them.

"On Earth, there are things called volcanoes. They're, like, giant openings in the ground. Occasionally, so much pressure would build up inside a volcano that it would explode, and the lava and the ash would kill everything around it."

The concept of volcanoes was familiar to Bastian, though he couldn't figure out why.

"So mountains that explode?" he asked.

Maeve nodded. "Yes. A long time ago, every volcano on Earth became active at the same time. They forced out so much magma that they drained the planet of its iron core."

"And what's the significance of that?" Bastian asked. He gripped the sheets spread over his legs. Since she'd begun her explanation, he'd nearly forgotten where he was.

"Our planet is constantly spinning. You don't feel it because of things such as gravity. But the Earth is able to spin because of its iron core. If it ever stops spinning, we'll all die." She said it so bluntly that Bastian wouldn't have been surprised if he learned she'd given this talk thousands of times. "When the scientists of Earth realized that all the volcanic activity would eventually cause the Earth to stop spinning, they came up with a plan: the nations of Earth would build two Totems that would keep the Earth spinning. That way, we'd never have to worry about extinction."

"And the ATP they mine from people who Level Up . . ." Bastian trailed off, waiting for her to complete his sentence for him.

"Goes to running Totem. Goes to making the Earth spin."

To Bastian, it all made sense. Though he didn't understand the details of Maeve's explanations, he grasped the concepts.

"So we're power generators raised for slaughter," Bastian said, staring at his bandaged hands.

"Precisely," Maeve said. "A perpetual machine that uses people like you as the power input. But we have to fix that. We need your help."

043:

Maeve helped Bastian to his feet and took him out of the room. He was still processing her words, trying to calm the raging emotions within him. He still hated himself for killing Simon. While he understood it was necessary, it still felt wrong to him.

The sensation of Simon's cold, bloody lips against his palm was stronger than the pain of the burn. And as if that wasn't enough for him to deal with, he'd been thrown into an entirely new world where all his friends who had ever Leveled Up had been turned into liquid and mined for their energy. He missed Odette and Callum, and he wished he knew how 55178 was doing. He hoped and hoped that they'd been able to connect someone to *Blissful Grocer* and get food.

To top off his emotional turmoil, Bastian was also starving. He didn't know hunger could be so voracious or so vast. His stomach felt bigger than his body, like it was nearing a point where it would turn on him and start feasting on him from the inside out. He wanted to ask for food, but he knew that was where Maeve was taking him. Earlier, she'd promised him a good meal.

"I'm part of a small team of rebels," Maeve explained as she led him out of the room. "This is where we camp. Sorry if they're a bit overwhelming. You are the first person we've retrieved from a town who is still alive."

Bastian gulped.

Maeve took him out the door and down a small hallway. Leaning against a wall at the end was an old bookshelf. Its decaying tomes were meager in size compared to the dust and the cobwebs.

"Here." Maeve grabbed a small book on the shelf and pulled it back. Something in the building groaned, and then the bookshelf swung away from the wall, revealing another room behind it. "Hidden door," she said, and she stepped through.

The strong scent of food was enough to make Bastian sick, but not enough to make him turn away. His body, while disgusted at ingesting any single thing, also understood how desperately it needed sustenance.

The room they stepped into was more like a massive auditorium. The floor was covered in rugs, the walls in cheap, floral tapestry, and the blinds were drawn, obscuring anyone's view outside or inside of the window.

A few people sat at desks, their backs turned to Bastian and Maeve as they worked away at their computers. Others noticed Maeve walk in, and they smiled at her. But when they saw Bastian, they quickly began whispering amongst each other.

"Here in the corner," Maeve said, pointing to a booth buried in the shadows.

He sat down, every limb and joint wobbling in protest of hunger, and as if on cue, a young woman appeared balancing a tray on one hand. "Here ya go, honey," she said, sliding the tray down in front of Bastian. "Don't eat it too fast, or it'll race out of you faster than you can put it back in."

He laughed, but he immediately thought of earlier that day when he'd thrown up in the room next to the Boss's office. Throwing up was sometimes necessary, but it was never ideal.

Condensation was dripping down the sides of the tray. Steam wafted up, sliding into Bastian's nose as if it were easing him into the meal. Before him was the most beautiful display of food he'd ever seen. He didn't understand what any of it was, so he pointed at Maeve and beckoned her over.

"Can you describe the food for me?" he asked. "I don't know what any of this is."

"I'd be happy to," she said, sliding into the bench across from him. "This here is steak." She pointed at a giant slab of what resembled meat. Bastian had only had meat once in his life before. Apparently, it was extremely difficult to find meat in *Blissful Grocer,* so Simon had never really bothered with it.

"These are called mashed potatoes, and these are carro—"

But her words were lost to Bastian's ears. He tore into the food with his bare hands, ignoring the utensils resting next to his plate, shoveling handfuls into his mouth. When he swallowed his first chunk of meat, his stomach literally groaned. By the third bite, he was already feeling so much better that he realized he'd forgotten how good it felt to have a full stomach.

"Why d'you guys 'ave dif'rent hair?" he asked as he chomped his food.

"You mean different-colored hair?" Maeve asked, pointing at her brown strands.

He nodded, swallowing another chunk of food.

"Redheads absorb ATP faster and better than any-body else," she said. "Personally, I don't know why, but I'm sure someone does."

"Lots of redheads," he said, taking a moment between bites to breathe.

"There's a reason for that," Maeve said. "For why there are only redheads in the towns."

"Hmm?" Bastian asked, taking a giant swig of water and diving into the carrots.

"You and everyone else from 55178 are clones."

044:

"I'm a clone?" The words came out dry even though his mouth was full of juicy food.

"You're a clone. One of many. As is everyone in 55178. Do you know what that is?"

"I don't think so." Bastian swallowed.

"It's a copy of a copy of a copy," Maeve said. "You have the same genes as everyone else."

Bastian nodded. He had heard of genetics and genes and did his best to wrap his mind around the whole thing.

Maeve held up two forks. "See how these are the same? Made of the same stuff?"

Bastian nodded again.

"That's what a clone is."

For the first time since he started eating, Bastian dropped his food and placed his hands by his plate. "I don't really understand," he said, even though he did. One of the very few fiction books he'd been read as a kid concerned clones. It was the full re-creation of a person. In the story, they were constructed in labs until they were sentient enough to exist without medical assistance. And yet, while he figured he should be devastated that he had no real parents, that he'd been born in a vial, that there were others *exactly* like him, it didn't fill him with any of the horror he'd expected. There was a calmness to this knowledge, a bliss. One he had never known in his life.

"You were created in a lab. Your pale skin, your red hair, your sensitivity to infrared light, it was all designed to make you the best conduit for ATP possible."

He didn't respond. Instead, he resumed devouring his meal.

"To be honest," Maeve said, biting at her fingernail, "I thought more of you would come."

"Hmm?"

"To help us shut down Totem. To help us put an end once and for all to the juicing process and return to the surface."

Bastian made some sort of sound, which Maeve interpreted perfectly. He had no idea what she was saying.

"Those messages I sent to you through the food boxes. I was hoping you would have brought more people with you."

"I'm not following," Bastian said. He finished the food on his plate and then began nibbling on the steak bone.

"Surely, you got my messages. The drawings. The letter. I explained all of it in the letter, what our plan was, why we needed more help." She found his eyes, though he was deep in thought, trying to remember every detail of the drawing.

Bastian began to protest, but then he remembered the blue folder he and Callum had found in Simon's office. Neither of them had gotten a chance to explore its contents. Maybe her letter was hidden in there. Maybe Simon, for some reason, had never shown them the letter.

"I'm not the one you were sending the messages to," Bastian admitted. She looked at him quizzically. He wiped his face with a napkin. "That was Simon. My friend Callum and I helped find the pieces to the drawing. Once it was completed, he Leveled Up. He never showed us a letter."

"He Leveled Up?" Maeve asked, clearly confused. "Why would he Level Up? I told him in the letter what happens to people when they Level Up." She paused, squinting her eyes. "He could read, right?"

"Yes," Bastian said. He, too, was confused why Simon had hidden the letter from him. But as soon as his suspicions grew, an obvious solution came to him.

"Simon was kind of paranoid," Bastian said. A lump formed in his throat, and he found it increasingly difficult to talk about his friend. "He was probably skeptical when he got the letter, and he didn't want to put any of us in danger in case it was a trap."

"So he Leveled Up knowing there was a possibility that he would be juiced on the other side?"

"No," Bastian said. "He took tools with him in the pod. I found him in the tunnel. He'd been bleeding out for almost three days. The only reason I came down after him was because he was linked to *Blissful Grocer*, and the town was beginning to starve." Bastian almost told Maeve what he'd done to Simon, what he'd been *forced to do* to Simon, but the words never found their way to his lips.

"Oh," Maeve said, and the conversation ended there.

They sat together in the booth for a while. Bastian leaned his head back against the seat and closed his eyes. Although the food was beginning to work its way into his system, he was still tired. Any amount of shut-eye he was able to snag was a treasure. In his half-slumber, half-wakefulness, he thought of Odette. He missed her. He'd never missed her before. He hated the feeling.

"I have a question," he announced, a thought suddenly occurring to him.

"Shoot," Maeve said. She, too, seemed to have drifted off.

"If your plan is to stop Totem, to stop the juicing process—which I'm all for, by the way—then won't the Earth stop rotating?"

"That's a long story," Maeve said. "But I'll give you the condensed version. Technically, yes, the Earth will stop spinning, and we'll all be launched off the surface of the planet. But theoretically, no. One of our guys claims to have been in contact with somebody from the Totem on the South Pole. They claimed they shut theirs down about a year ago because iron had returned to the Earth's core, and it no longer needed help spinning. I believe him, and so does everybody else helping us."

"Isn't that risky?" Bastian asked. "Betting the whole planet on a rumor?"

"Yes," Maeve said. Bastian was surprised by her honesty. It impressed him. "But what's worse: killing off the human race, or allowing the human race to continue growing babies in labs whose sole purpose is to be slaughtered for their energy?"

Bastian didn't answer her question. He assumed it was rhetorical.

She made a good point.

045:

Before Bastian drifted off into sleep entirely, Maeve grabbed him by the hand and took him to another spiral staircase hidden in a closet just a few feet away from them. Her hand felt weird in his. Not in a physical sense, but in an emotional one. All he could think about were Odette's hands.

The staircase led to an attic. It was roomy, probably the size of the Arcade aside from its slanted roof. Cots lined the walls, and a few people were already tucked under the covers, snoring.

"This is where we sleep," Maeve said. "Your bed is the one in the back there. The sun will set in less than an hour." She paused, chewing on the inside of her cheek. "I'm not trying to send you to bed or anything like that. You just look exhausted."

"No," Bastian said, "I am tired. Thank you." Not only was he just tired, but his stomach was full of warm food. He knew he'd be out cold the moment his head hit a pillow.

She began to walk away, but he grabbed her elbow,

stopping her. "Why are you doing all this for me?" he asked.

"Even if you refuse to help, we're going to stop Totem. For all we know, it may end the world. Might as well make everyone's possibly last days some good ones."

✳✳✳

Bastian dreamt that night. Not about giants roaming an uninhabited Earth beyond the concrete walls of 55178, but about standing on the ground of a scorched Earth as liquified fire continued to roll over it, eventually engulfing him and turning him into ash.

Bastian woke to a flurry of hushed voices. He was pressed deep into his mattress, as if gravity was working twice as hard on him. He hadn't shifted an inch the entire night, and his muscles and bones protested when he began to move. But he couldn't remember the last time he'd felt this good—if he ever had. The only thing bothering him was the familiar ache of hunger in his stomach.

"Finally awake?" Maeve asked, appearing next to his bed. Her long brown hair was pulled into a bun. "Come and meet everyone."

Before he could say no, she grabbed him by the hand once again and pulled him out of bed. A dozen people sat in a circle on the floor on the other side of the room. A diagram was laid out in front of them, the edges held down by devices with what looked like joysticks attached to the top.

Maeve sat down and patted the empty spot next to her. Bastian took a seat. He was still waking up.

"Bastian, this is the rebellion."

"I thought there'd be more of you," he said, echoing Maeve's words from the day before.

"Oh, there are more of us. Hundreds more," a dark-skinned man across from Bastian said. He had an afro of black hair, and the beginnings of a beard were speckling his jawline. "They've already been given their assignments for the day."

"Ah," Bastian said. He was relieved by the words, though. Maeve had neglected to mention that the plan to take down Totem involved hundreds of people. Including the clones from the various towns.

"I'm Dacens, by the way," the dark-skinned man mentioned. He seemed to only be a few years older than Bastian himself, as did everyone else in the group. Come to think of it, Bastian didn't remember seeing a single older adult since Maeve brought him here.

"Dacens is the one who drew the diagram I sent you," Maeve explained.

"I assume Maeve has filled you in on all the intimate details?" Dacens asked.

"Not really," she said. "But he knows the mission, and he's willing to help. Right?" She looked at him, her casual smile now forced down into a concerned line.

"Of course," Bastian said. What choice did he have?

"Good man," said a bald woman in the group.

"Maeve," Dacens said, pointing at someplace on the map, "you and Bastian will cover the juicer. That's this area." With his finger, he circled a part of the map. Bastian figured it was a map of Hub City, but he didn't recognize any of the roads or the structures. "Before you leave, I'll give you a smaller map indicating where you place the bombs."

"Bombs?" Bastian asked. Nobody had said anything about bombs.

"Yes, bombs," Dacens said. "If you place them—"

"Probably not the bombs you know," Maeve said, interrupting him.

"EMPs," said another woman in the group. She had a small frame and short blonde hair.

"E-bombs," Dacens explained. "Electromagnetic pulses. They don't blow anything up. They just wipe out all electronics within a certain radius. Theoretically, there shouldn't be any casualties."

Dacens grabbed one of the joysticks holding down the edges of the unfurled map. When he picked it up, the map rolled up. He held the joystick for everyone to see. It was attached to a small box with a red button and a blue button on either side of it.

"To stick these to the walls, you pull off this flap here." He pointed at a thin layer of plastic coating the bottom of the box. "It'll stick to any flat surface. To arm the bombs, you hold it so the red button is on your left and the blue button is on your right, like this. Then you move it up, up, down, down, left, right, left, right, and then push both buttons at the same time." He demonstrated the actions. Bastian recognized the similar pattern from when Thayer would run a new spawning on a game.

"Is everyone clear on this?" Dacens asked.

Everyone except Bastian nodded their heads. Everything was moving so fast. He'd barely had time to process all the answers Maeve had given him the day before, and now he was about to help destroy a giant machine spinning the planet.

"Great," Dacens said. "But first, let's eat. Don't want to save the world on empty stomachs."

046:

Bastian, Maeve, Dacens, and the bald woman, whose name was Lessit, sat at the same booth where Bastian had eaten his steak the day before. The rest of the group was scattered throughout the cafeteria. Today, they'd been served what Maeve called burgers. It was meat smashed between two pieces of bread. It sounded disgusting, but Bastian thought it might be the best thing he'd ever tasted.

"How long does it take for your food to go bad?" he asked. He figured it took a different amount of time. It had to.

"Depends on the food," Dacens explained. "Generally, if you refrigerate it—er, keep it cold—it'll last quite a while. If you left your burger here on the table, it'd probably take a matter of hours."

"So not everything goes bad within twenty-four hours?"

"No," Lessit said. She'd barely touched her meal. Bastian wondered if she was nervous about their mission. "There's a food from Earth called manna. It has an expiration date of twenty-four hours. When scientists designed

Totem, they decided almost everything, not just the food, would need to act like manna. Nearly everything sent to you from playing the games was bioengineered to disintegrate within a day. Their theory was it would force the citizens of the towns to rely on the gamers, and the gamers would thus be pressured to continue playing the games and continue to Level Up. It also stopped hierarchies from forming in most of the towns, as it was impossible to hoard any resource."

"It didn't stop *every* town from going completely nuts," Dacens said. "Just last year, the Boss had to send some people up to eliminate the inhabitants of 376616. Apparently, the gamers forced other citizens to do some, uh, messed up things. I won't share the specifics; it would make you sick."

"Who is the Boss?" Bastian asked. "I saw him when I first got here. He looked—"

"You *saw* him?" Maeve asked. Her mouth fell open, as did Lessit's and Dacens's.

Bastian took another bite of his burger, and then with a full mouth, asked, "Is that bad?"

"Nobody has ever seen him," Lessit said. "At least, none of us have. We don't even know where he stays. He's so secretive that some people are convinced he's a myth. Maybe even a clone himself."

"Well, the guy I saw was real," Bastian said. His stomach was once again full. Now that the hunger was fading, he realized how badly he truly did stink. If he didn't get a shower soon, his skin would probably start rotting off his bones. "And the blue-suit people referred to him as the Boss."

"What does he look like?" Dacens asked. His full lips had pulled back in a grin, revealing dazzling white teeth. He was excited, vibrating with ecstatic energy.

"He was huge," Bastian said. "Really tall, really big, huge arms. I never got to see his face, but he was still scary."

"Where'd you see him?" Dacens asked.

"Two guys pulled a woman out of one of the pods and knocked her out." He swallowed the last of his food, eyeing Lessit's untouched burger. "I followed them down and to the Boss's office. Obviously, none of them saw me, but I spied on them through the blinds."

"What did he do with the woman?" Lessit asked, running her hand over her shining head.

"He was looking at her neck or her face or something. Then he said 'not her' and the guys took her away."

"Well, that all but confirms it," Maeve said, wiping her hands on her shirt.

"Confirms what?"

"There's something you need to understand about our organization," Dacens replied. "We formed a few years ago, but our ideology has existed for nearly a decade. The first scientist to suggest it was time to begin considering ending Totem did so nearly twelve years ago. Rumor has it he caused such an uproar that the Boss got involved. Shortly after, the scientist mysteriously went missing."

"The Boss killed him," Maeve said, and nobody disagreed with her.

"Apparently, that scientist knew the Boss was coming after him. So in an effort to preserve his own life, he kidnapped the Boss's daughter and sent her to one of the towns. Turns out, it didn't save his life in the end. And I guess the Boss has been looking for her ever since. I heard that early on, he even went into each city to look for her."

"Interesting," Bastian remarked.

"Well," Dacens said, glancing about the cafeteria. "If you guys are ready, I think it's time we head out."

"Head out for what?" Bastian asked.

"For the EMP stuff," Maeve said.

"That's happening today?" Bastian asked. He'd thought he would have at least another day to review the plans. He hadn't prepared himself to do it today.

"Everything is already set in motion," Dacens said. "It has to be today, unless you have a really good reason otherwise."

"Honestly, I do," Bastian said. "I desperately need a shower."

047:

The shower was resplendent. It was in the back of the bookstore on the main floor. Apparently, it was a communal shower and rarely available, but Bastian had asked to take one in the rare time that it was free. He wanted to stay under the steady stream of hot, clean water for longer than he did, but he knew a dozen people were waiting on him, that a plan to either end or save the world was waiting for the moment he stepped out of his shower. So he hurried.

When he stepped out of the shower, he found a fresh pair of clothes waiting for him next to the sink. It was the same blue uniform he'd seen the workers from the factory wearing. He slipped them on, his skin rejoicing at the clean fabric, and returned to the bookstore's attic.

"Now, are we all ready?" Dacens asked.

Everyone nodded, including Bastian. "Do I need to cover my hair?"

"Nah," Maeve said. "Redheads aren't dominate in Hub City, but we still have a few."

"All right," Dacens said, addressing the group, "we'll

all set out in pairs. Is everyone clear on their assigned areas?" Everyone nodded. "Good. Each pair will receive a backpack with six bombs and a map. Activate the bombs the way I showed you, and then return here. I won't detonate them until we've all safely returned. Does that sound like a plan?"

Everybody murmured in agreement.

"Then get going."

✳✳✳

"Where are we headed?" Bastian asked once he and Maeve had left the bookstore. They both wore blue uniforms. He assumed it would help them blend in with whatever location they were covering.

"We got the worst one, remember?" Maeve said, tightening the backpack's straps. "The juicer."

"Will we see any of it?" Bastian asked, fearing the answer.

"Yes. And I'm sorry. It's . . . brutal. Hopefully, you won't see the worst of it, but I doubt you'll be able to avoid it entirely."

Hub City looked different to Bastian now that he was well-rested, well-fed, and well-cleaned. The sky was bluer, the air crisper, and the colors were more vibrant. What he found most odd about the city was the lack of looming concrete walls. The horizon stretched farther than he could see. He felt free, but in a strange, unnatural way.

"What's your story, Maeve?" Bastian asked. They were nearing the edge of the abandoned area, about to emerge into the alleyways hidden from the bustling streets.

"It's not very exciting," she warned, sighing. Her eyes were brighter in the sunlight. The rich brown was now a glimmering bronze. For some reason, when he looked at her, he thought of Odette. It made him feel guilty, and he wasn't sure why.

"I was born here, went to school, learned about Totem and why humans left the Earth's surface. A few years ago, my parents died in a factory accident. It was awful." She swallowed, and Bastian ignored the tears building up at the corners of her eyes. "I was just friends with Dacens at the time. We'd gone to school together. When he heard about the accident, he came and found me. One thing led to another, and now I'm here."

"That's . . . I'm sorry," Bastian said, unsure what to say. Outside of the occasional sacrifice, death was a rare event in 55178. Aside from Milt, he hadn't personally known anyone who had died, just recognized their name when their burning was announced.

"Death is part of life," she said. "And I know this may be a twisted way of looking at things, but that's how I made peace with Dacens's plan to bomb Totem. I was on the fence for weeks, and then one day, he told me, 'Maeve, death is a part of life. Either it was time for life on Earth to end when the volcanoes went off, and we're helping nature take its course, or we'll survive. Either way, death will eventually find us all.'"

"Hmm," Bastian murmured, replaying the words in his mind, examining how he felt about them.

"Why did you agree?" Maeve asked. "To all of this, I mean?"

He didn't struggle to answer the question. "It just feels right," he replied.

They entered an alleyway. It was cooler here in the shade. He took a moment to appreciate the weather. In 55178, there was one temperature, and it was blazing hot. Here, though, the weather seemed to change frequently.

"You smell good, by the way," Maeve remarked as they stepped out onto a sidewalk swarming with other people. "Much better than before."

Bastian smiled. He liked Maeve. He thought Callum would like her, too. Maybe soon, they would meet.

Bastian followed Maeve down a number of different streets. He was entranced by each building they passed. Every single one was different from the last, and none of them resembled any from 55178. He was most excited whenever they walked by windows. Many of them weren't covered, and he was able to see inside. There were buildings filled just with clothing, others with food, some with furniture. Many of them carried an assortment of items.

"Do people live in these?" Bastian asked, gesturing to the buildings around them.

"No. These are stores. This is where people buy things."

He didn't respond. Frankly, he was tired of asking questions, and he suspected Maeve was tired of answering them. But she must have seen the puzzled look on his face, because she explained further. "People here have something called money. It's something we earn through doing jobs like, for example, stocking shelves. We then use the money we earn to buy things we need or want, like food and clothes and games."

"So you don't just get food? You have to earn it?"

"Exactly."

"That seems awful," Bastian said. "What if you can't earn it? Or what if you don't have enough money to buy food?"

"Then you starve." She held her hands up by her head.

"Sounds unfair," he said.

"That's what some people think," she said.

They walked in silence for another ten minutes. Bastian continued looking through every window they passed, and Maeve simply watched him. It wasn't until they were nearly thirty minutes away from the bookstore that Maeve held out her hand and stopped Bastian.

"There it is," she said, pointing ahead. Across the street, a tall spire rose into the sky. It resembled a knife. The sight of it triggered something primal in Bastian, and his stomach twisted in response.

"Follow me," Maeve said. "Let's get this over with."

048:

For some reason, Bastian had assumed they were going to sneak into the building, but Maeve led him straight through the front door. Inside, the building was dark. The windows had been tinted, and very little sunlight managed to get in. Dull lights hanging from the ceiling by chains did little to illuminate the corners of the front room.

"Good morning!"

The voice startled Bastian. He'd been too busy taking in his bland surroundings to notice a desk on the other side of the room. A woman with blonde hair and bronze skin sat on a chair on the opposite side of the desk. A monitor rested in front of her, casting a glowing blue light across her sharp features.

"Good morning," Maeve said. "Just headed to the third floor. Training, you know? Ugh."

The blonde woman smiled. Some kind of metal track lined both rows of her teeth. Bastian refrained from examining her mouth further, even though he'd never seen anything like it.

"Oh, believe me, I understand your pain. I worked there for one day before I decided I'd rather die than do it. I'll never understand how you people do that job."

"Pays well," Maeve said, shrugging. She pushed Bastian toward a chrome double door.

The blonde woman made a face, and Maeve nodded. They may as well have been speaking in made-up words. Bastian hadn't understood a single letter of that conversation.

The silver doors slid open, and Bastian stepped inside. He was surprised to find they led into an extremely small room, but then Maeve stepped in behind him and pressed a button numbered "3."

"This is an elevator," he said.

"Yeah," she said. "It takes people up and down floors. Saves them a trip up the stairs."

Once again, Bastian thought of 55178. He couldn't wait to tell Odette and Callum all that had happened to him. He hoped that he could one day bring them here to visit, to show them the cool buildings, the great food, and the people he'd met.

If all goes to plan today, Bastian thought, *it won't be long until I see them again.*

The elevator lurched, and then gravity seemed to grow in strength. He barely had time to respond to the situation before the elevator came to a stop. The doors slid open, revealing an entirely different floor than the one below. This one resembled the place he'd first arrived in; however, it was much busier and seemed smaller.

Tons of people also donning the same blue uniforms passed by them, talking to others around them or staring down at the clipboards in their hands. The floor was made of the same metal grating. Maeve pulled him out of the elevator, and together they headed right.

Bastian clung to Maeve's hand as they fought the flow of the crowd. Once again, nobody paid them any attention. Everybody seemed preoccupied. The farther away they got from the elevators, the more Bastian realized they were headed toward heavy machinery. Whirring, clanking, and shouting helped him understand what kind of situation they were about to enter before he even caught a glimpse of it. Then, moments later, they emerged under a concrete archway into a massive, domed room. On their left, stairs crawled up a series of staggered platforms. On these platforms, some people stood, glancing between their handheld screens and whatever was in front of them. Some sat at desks, where they clacked away at keyboards. Others were gathered in circles, talking amongst themselves. Bastian estimated there were at least two hundred people altogether on the platforms.

To their right, the wall was covered by gargantuan windows. And when Bastian saw what was going on behind the glass, he nearly threw up.

The ceiling was lined with a snaking track that was constantly moving. Attached to the track were giant claws. And hanging upside down from the claws were limp, unconscious people.

Bastian watched in horror as the claws moved slowly along the track, the bodies swinging as if blown about by a light breeze. Some of the bodies twitched as the track slid them along. Bastian kept his eyes trained on one of the bodies, a male about his age with the same red hair. Near the end of the track, the claw opened, and the body fell into what resembled a giant, clear cup. Moments later, something within the giant cup spun to life, and within seconds, the person was sliced into pieces. Blood, flesh, and bone splattered the sides of the container. Water sprayed from spouts lining the rim of the giant cup, and the gore quickly washed to the bottom.

To Bastian's utter disgust, the process didn't end there. About half a minute later, a small conveyer belt below the container came to life, and a tray containing the remnants of the body appeared. It was all mush now, all liquid. The conveyer belt took it through a square opening in the wall, and then it disappeared from sight.

He watched two more bodies get sliced into juice before Maeve grabbed his arm and led him away.

049:

"Here," Maeve said, pointing to the nearest corner. Nobody in the room was paying them attention, and Bastian was trying his hardest to keep his eyes averted from the juicer. It was the most disgusting, inhumane thing he had ever seen. To think that had most recently happened to Dr. Soren, and had almost happened to Simon . . . He placed a hand over his mouth. Now, he was grateful he'd killed Simon. If he hadn't, the poor gamer would be juice by now.

Bastian reached into Maeve's backpack and swiftly pulled out the EMP. He removed the adhesive strip on the bottom and pressed it against the corner near the floor where people were less likely to see it. Without waiting for Maeve's order, Bastian moved the joystick up, up, down, down, left, right, left, right, and then pushed both buttons at the same time.

Nothing happened. He moved to make sure he'd done it right, but a dim red light near the joystick began blinking. It was armed. He got to his feet, double-checked that nobody had noticed them, and then left the room with Maeve.

They repeated this four more times without incident, placing each bomb in a different room. Nobody glanced twice at them while the facility was filled with employees milling about. It appeared as though nobody was particularly interested in anyone else. And judging by the paperwork Bastian saw them doing, nobody seemed interested in the labor either.

When Maeve led Bastian into another room to place the sixth and final bomb, he immediately found the space eerie and oddly quiet.

The room was as large as the cafeteria in 55178. The walls were concrete and bare, and the floor was lined with steel rows of shelves. At first, Bastian thought they were filing cabinets—he'd seen a few of those in 55178—but he quickly realized they were far too large to be filing cabinets.

"I've heard of this place," Maeve said. Her voice was quiet and cold. "I didn't know it would be here."

"What do you mean?" Bastian asked.

"It's marked as a maintenance room. That's just . . . that's *sick*."

Maeve's face was contorted, as if her body was struggling between crying and throwing up. Realizing he wasn't about to get an answer from her, Bastian stepped into the nearest aisle.

He froze. His heart seemed to stop beating.

"Oh," he said, his voice more of a stuttering breath.

The steel rows weren't shelves at all, nor were they filing cabinets. The front was covered entirely by thick glass, so everything within was visible. And what Bastian saw filled him with so many emotions and feelings at once—anger, confusion, nausea, hatred—that he wasn't sure how to process everything before him.

The glass was divided every three feet by another pane. And in each one of those spaces was a person. They were standing, their shoulders squeezed by the glass, with not even enough room to sit down. All of them seemed exhausted, the type of exhaustion that was born from an overpowering, overwhelming fear.

Bastian nearly failed to recognize the most startling observation. Everyone here had red hair. Everyone here was a clone just like him.

The girl in front of him was no older than him. Her red hair was cut short like a boy's, and it was unkempt and frazzled. She had freckles just like Odette that bridged her nose. Dark bags rimmed her eyes, and she stood slumped over like she was taking a nap standing up. When she noticed Bastian, she simply blinked at him as if he were nothing but a dream.

"Maeve," Bastian demanded. "What is this place?"

Maeve stepped up next to him. She avoided looking at anyone. "These are the people they use to create clones." She pointed at the exposed arms of the girl in front of them. "See those scars? That's where they remove tissue. If you could see under her shirt, you'd find even more. They take patches of skin, bits of organ, vials of blood—they take everything from these people to build clones. Eventually, they die."

"There are dozens of them," Bastian said. He couldn't fully comprehend what Maeve had just told him. He had known cruelty in 55178. He'd seen it many times. He'd even dealt it once or twice. But this around him reached beyond the deepest depths of cruelty he had ever imagined. It was . . . it was *evil*.

The word rang true in his mind. He'd learned it as a

child, but it was never used in 55178. It applied to noth-ing there. But this place was most evil, and somehow his beating heart—the same one Odette had listened to—knew it.

He'd spent his entire life imagining the wonders that lay beyond the walls of his home. He'd dreamed of great people, of an amazing society that valued all and helped those in need. He'd dreamed of a world better than his own. But everything about this place was worse. From the moment he'd stepped out of the Elevator to this very moment, he'd been living in a nightmare.

"We have to set them free," Bastian said. It was the first thing he'd said with confidence since leaving 55178. He knew Maeve understood his implication. He wasn't going to leave until everybody could.

"Okay," she agreed, nodding her head. "Okay. But how do we—"

The door squealed as it opened.

Bastian and Maeve dove behind the cells and pressed their backs flat against them. Someone had entered the room. Or was it two people?

Bastian's muscles tensed as the footsteps grew louder, and Maeve reached out and grabbed his hand. If they were caught, they'd have virtually no chance of escaping.

The footsteps stopped.

"This one, sir?" The voice was meager and quiet.

Cautiously, his entire body shaking with fear, Bastian peered around the corner of the cellblock. Two men stood with their backs to him, facing one of the prisoners. The glass panel had slid halfway open, and the girl behind it had scrunched up her face. The scrawny man reached into the cell, his hands obscured by his body.

But it was none of that that had Bastian concerned. It was the other man, the silent giant.

He was enormous, looming; even his shadow appeared as a bottomless abyss.

It was the Boss.

050:

Maeve yanked Bastian out of view. Surprisingly, his trembling had stopped. He was calm. He knew what they had to do.

"The smaller guy can open the cells," Bastian said, whispering to her in his quietest voice. "You take him."

"What are you going to do?" she asked. Bastian realized she hadn't seen either of the men who now stood only a few yards away from them.

"The Boss is here," Bastian said. He didn't give her time to respond. "I'll take him. You get all of these people out of here."

"Bastian!" Maeve hissed, but he ignored her, slipped out of her grip, and snatched the backpack off her shoulders.

When he stepped into view, he expected some kind of stunned silence, but instead, he was met with no response at all. The Boss and the man next to him hadn't even heard him. Or if they had, they weren't paying him any attention. Their backs were still turned.

Bastian cleared his throat, coughing into a closed fist.

Both of them turned around, startled, but not scared. And for the first time, Bastian found himself face-to-face with the Boss.

He was bald, and the shining skin of his forehead continued down around his eyes. A spotty, black beard began at his cheekbones and extended an inch below his chin. Twisting the skin of his left temple was a gnarly scar. It pulled his entire face off-center.

"Who are you?" the other man asked. He had long, curly gray hair. His gloved hands rested on the glass, a sharp instrument in one of them. All the prisoners lifted their heads to catch a view of Bastian.

"Name's Bastian," he said.

"And what are you doing here, Bastian?" the Boss asked. He spoke out the side of his mouth in a low, gravelly tone.

"I'm here to stop you." He reached into the backpack and pulled out the EMP. "This is a bomb," he said, taking one step forward. "If you don't leave right now, I'll kill all of us."

The Boss chuckled, and the man next to him did, too. "I don't believe you," the Boss said.

Bastian moved the toggle on the EMP—up, up, down, down, left, right, left, and right—then pressed both buttons simultaneously. When he was done, the blinking red light appeared. The Boss looked to his associate, who nodded in confirmation.

"You won't get out of here alive," the Boss said.

"Neither will you unless you leave right now." Bastian lifted the bomb higher in the air. Its flashing light cast a sickly red along the glass.

The Boss moved forward, but Bastian placed his finger on top of the blue button. He knew, of course, that there would be no detonation, not even an electronic one.

As far as he was aware, he couldn't trigger that function from the device itself.

"Don't test me," Bastian said.

The associate leaned toward the Boss and whispered, "I don't think he's bluffing. We'll go and call security. They won't make it out of the building."

The Boss nodded, smiling at Bastian. "Be seeing you."

They turned to leave, but Bastian coughed again and held his free hand out. "I'll be needing the key," he said, "to these cells. Of course, you wouldn't mind. After all, you're so certain we can't make it out of here."

"Give it to him," the Boss demanded, and Bastian's stomach nearly exploded in shock.

The associate tossed him a smaller version of the handheld screen others had been carrying around. Then he and the Boss walked backward until they were out the door and out of sight.

"How in the *world* did that just happen?" Maeve asked, appearing from around the corner.

Bastian held the screen in his hand, trying to understand what exactly had just happened, too. He'd expected to fight, for things to get bloody. Instead, the Boss had just rolled over like a wounded animal.

"Maybe this happens more frequently than we think," Bastian said, "and it's never an issue."

"Maybe," Maeve said. She snatched the screen from Bastian's hands and began tapping it. He saw images, numbers, and dials flicker past the screen, but he didn't pay too much attention. He was more focused on the people imprisoned behind the glass.

Moments later, something *hissed*. Then the glass panels imprisoning the tired and weak people slipped into the ground. The first few stepped out of their cells, disbelief evident in their eyes. They hunched over, stared at their hands, and glanced left and right as if everything around them was fragile and would shatter at the slightest breath.

"Give me the bomb," Maeve instructed, holding out her hands. Her face was drenched in sweat, and Bastian realized for the first time how hot it was in the room.

"Why?"

"I'm going to activate the detonation now," Maeve said as she pressed one of the buttons.

"You can do that?" he asked.

"Yeah."

"But Dacens said he—"

"Dacens lied because he didn't want anyone getting spooked and detonating too early." She continued fiddling with the EMP as the prisoners poured from their cells, life returning to their grim faces.

"Thing is," Maeve said, "the Boss probably has a whole security team waiting for us just outside. There's no chance we make it more than five feet before we're all killed. Unless you have a better plan, I think our only chance at escape is detonating this."

Bastian wanted to argue. The idea of being inside a building targeted by multiple EMPs left him unsettled, but he didn't have a plan. Maeve was right. In his undeniable need to free the people here, he'd also trapped them.

"When these things go off, we need to run. Hopefully, it will cause enough confusion for us to get away unnoticed," she said.

"Okay," Bastian said. "I'm with you." He was still trying to process his feelings and his thoughts, but everything was moving too fast for him. More and more people were leaving their cells, finally understanding that this wasn't a trap or a trick.

"Listen up!" Maeve shouted. All the prisoners paused

and looked at her. "We're here to save you, but we need you to follow us. When I detonate this"—she held the EMP in the air—"it's gonna get very confusing for everybody out there." She pointed to the door. "You'll need to follow us, and you'll need to be fast. Understand?"

Bastian knew that not everyone was within sight, but everyone had definitely heard Maeve. She was so loud in such a quiet room.

"You ready?" she asked Bastian, and he nodded. Then she pressed the button, and the blinking red light on the EMP went dark.

051:

Bastian expected a loud noise like a heartbeat, but instead only heard a quick snippet of static. It fizzled, then faded.

"Did it work?" he asked. But Maeve didn't need to answer his question because, at that moment, the lights went out. The room was thrown into total darkness. People shouted just beyond the door, startled by the sudden disappearance of all light.

"Let's go!" Maeve shouted.

Ahead of them, someone opened the door. A dusky light filtered through. It wasn't very illuminating, but it was at least enough to go by.

Maeve pushed to the front of the crowd, and Bastian followed closely behind her. They left the room, checking over their shoulders to ensure the prisoners were following. They moved sluggishly, still exhausted from the countless experiments done on them. But at least they were on their feet.

They entered into the same hallway as before. It was vacant and would've been entirely dark if it weren't for the high-up windows allowing the evening light through.

"This way," Maeve said.

They went left down the hallway, retracing their same steps as before. Bastian kept his eye out for the Boss or any armed guards the whole time. Like Maeve, he was confident the Boss was waiting for them somewhere, and he probably wouldn't be afraid to hurt them.

When they reached the end of the hallway, Maeve paused and pressed her back against the wall. She breathed slowly as everyone came to a stop behind her.

"We've got this," Bastian said, surprised still by his newfound confidence. "It's now or never."

She nodded, then rounded the corner.

Lining the room between them and the door were a dozen guards. They held guns with long barrels that required two hands to shoot. The shots started instantly. Bastian felt the bullets whiz past his head before he heard the gunfire. Maeve ducked, yanking him down with her. Plaster and glass rained down upon them. They crawled forward, flinching as bullets flew over their heads, and the prisoners they'd set free ran toward the assailants, determined to get their revenge. A prisoner fell down next to them. He was limp, a bullet hole centered directly on his forehead.

"We're not going to get past them," Maeve said. She was sweating, and her cheek was cut open. The windows in the room had all been shattered by the bullets, and Bastian realized bits of it had embedded into his palm. A trail of blood followed him.

Bastian knew what Maeve had said was right. They would both die here. He only became surer of it every time he heard a bullet fire and saw another body drop. They'd led these people right into slaughter. He thought of Simon, of how peaceful he'd looked when Bastian had killed him. He thought of the poor people dying around him, how desperate they'd looked in their cages, and how empty their corpses looked now.

So much death. His whole life, he'd unknowingly been surrounded by it, held up just high enough in the sky so he wouldn't drown. But now, here he was, lying as still as possible to avoid becoming another dead body in the heap.

Bastian's thoughts were yanked away from him when the wall to his right exploded. Chunks of concrete blew sideways, knocking out a few of the gunmen and cracking the floor. Ears ringing, heart racing, dust stinging his eyes, Bastian searched for the source of the explosion. The gunmen were still firing, but they were blinded as well, and their bullets bounced uselessly off nearby walls. The prisoners who'd survived the spray of bullets pushed in closer to Maeve, who was huddled next to Bastian, her hands over her head.

A figure emerged from the smoke. Judging by his size, he was a teenager.

"Who's that?" Maeve asked, her neck craned back to see. Bastian shrugged and lifted his head a little higher, finally above the thick cloud of dust.

"Callum?"

"Everybody down!" Callum shouted. He raised his arm in the air and brought it down like an ax. Then he dove next to Bastian and the others.

"Callum?" Bastian asked again. "Is that really you?"

"Sure is, buddy," Callum said. He flashed a huge smile and wrapped Bastian in a hug. He wore a sleeveless shirt, and the concrete dust had clung to his sweaty forehead, making him appear paler than usual.

"Wha—"

"Read those pages we found in Simon's drawer," Callum explained. He seemed so odd to Bastian at that moment, so out of place. But he was still Callum through and through, joyful, oblivious, and a much-needed boost of energy. "Gave instructions on what was going on down here and how to stop it. Once I realized you might get juiced, I came as fast as I could."

Bastian stuttered, the words he wanted to say only getting caught in his throat. He was simultaneously flooded with shock and relief.

The sudden sound of another bullet spray echoed off the concrete chunks surrounding them. Bastian clamped his bandaged hands over his ears. To his surprise, he realized the gunfire was coming from his right and that the gunmen were all being targeted, dropping into lifeless clumps.

"What's going on?" Maeve asked.

Callum smiled at her. "I'm Callum. You must be Maeve. I read your letter."

Maeve smiled back, then he looked to Bastian. "It was in Simon's blue folder."

"Okay," Maeve said. "How did you find us?"

"Dacens and his crew were waiting close by," Callum answered. "When you set off the EMPs, he knew something was wrong. All of us came here to save you."

Like it'd been planned, the faint silhouettes of dozens of people appeared outside the hole in the wall. They held guns pressed into their shoulders, still trained on the room.

Dacens appeared. He was dressed in cargo pants and a vest with many pockets. He, too, held a gun. "Come on, guys," he said, looking down at them. "It's time we get everybody home."

052:

Callum grabbed Bastian by the arm and lifted him up. "How are your hands doing?" he asked.

"Fine, I think," Bastian said. To be honest, he wasn't sure how they felt. The ringing in his ears and the deep ache in his muscles from the explosion were at the forefront of his sensations.

Callum pulled Bastian toward the hole he'd blown in the side of the building. He watched as Maeve found Dacens, and the two began guiding the prisoners where to go. He looked away when he saw all the bodies strewn across the floor—prisoners and assailants. Some were riddled with bullet holes, others were crushed by concrete.

"I told them I came here to find you," Callum said. Bastian wasn't sure if his friend had just begun talking or if he'd been speaking for a while. "While Simon's papers did a good job at explaining Totem and what was going on, they helped fill in some of the holes."

He and Bastian crested the last chunk of concrete and emerged into the evening air. A line of individuals—all of whom Bastian recognized from the bookstore—stood at the ready with their guns, surveying the area. In the distance, people fled the industrial buildings of Hub City, headed toward their homes.

"It's crazy, isn't it?" Callum said. But Bastian didn't respond. "All of this. Last week, you and I were stocking shelves, only imagining what could be beyond the walls. Now we're about to take down the industry that's been killing different versions of us for generations."

"I haven't even begun to process it," Bastian said. To assure himself that he wasn't imagining things, he reached out and grabbed Callum by the arm. His skin was warm, and the cement dust that covered it was rough, but he was sure enough real.

"How's Simon?" Callum asked. They stopped on the sidewalk. Above them, the moon shone down, washing the street in a warm blue light.

Bastian frowned, his gut folding in on itself. Ever since he'd sacrificed Simon, he'd feared answering this question. He didn't want to answer it. He didn't want Callum or Odette or anyone else to look at him differently. Sacrifices in 55178 were different. It was the doctor's duty to kill them with grace. They injected them with a poison that put them slowly into a forever sleep. But Bastian had killed Simon with his bare hands. He'd looked into Simon's eyes as the life faded from them. He'd felt his very last hot breath against his palm.

"I take it he didn't make it?" Callum asked.

Bastian couldn't bring himself to tell the truth, so he just nodded. A moment of silence passed between them. Silence was never natural for Callum. It never existed around him. This was his way of giving Simon one last notion of respect.

"How's Odette?" Bastian asked. Dacens and Maeve

had funneled most of the survivors from the building, and those standing guard were readying to leave.

"About that . . ." Callum said.

Bastian's heart dropped.

"I think you're going to see her much sooner than you expect."

"What does that mean?" Bastian asked.

Before Callum could respond, Dacens interrupted them. He shouted, but his voice didn't carry very far. "Before the EMPs were detonated, I managed to send out a command to every town connected to Hub City." He held up a screen. Giant, bolded letters appeared across it.

?syntax error system.out.in (hello world)

"The automatic doors on the Bins where their food and other necessities are delivered have been deactivated, they can open and close them at will—no more threat of being chopped in half. They will be notified of this on their Arcade game consoles. The Bins will deliver the townspeople to the center of Hub City, at the exportation building. We only have a short amount of time before the Boss mobilizes his resources against us, so I suggest we hurry."

Dacens jumped down from the wall and began jogging toward the street.

"Hey," Bastian called out, holding up his hand, "where are we going? I mean after we get everyone, where are we going?"

"To Earth," Dacens replied.

✖✖✖

Hub City was a field of chaos. Citizens ran from one place to another, shouting and chattering, attempting to uncover the mystery as to why every electronic within city limits suddenly went out. While Bastian hated the presence of people he knew would rat them out to the Boss in one second flat, he was grateful for how many there were. He, Callum, Maeve, Dacens, and the people they'd saved had so far gone unnoticed.

They wound through the crowd like a long coil, constantly swiveling and swerving, somehow never breaking formation.

"Not too far from here," Dacens said. He led the group, and Bastian was just behind him. The buildings loomed far above them, their tops blending in with the dark clouds. The moon faded in and out of view, consistently showering Hub City in a blanket of darkness before illuminating its roads and rooftops.

Bastian knew they were close to the center of Hub City when he began catching glimpses of red hair. They were like sparks of fire, flames of hope. Every time, he double-checked for Odette. The last thing he wanted to do was miss her because he wasn't concentrating hard enough.

Then Dacens came to a stop.

The crowd had stopped moving. Men, women, and children stood in a half-circle around the entrance of a building. A sign labeled it as "EXPORTATION." The same building Bastian exited to this strange new world just yesterday. Redheaded individuals filed out the door. They clumped together, holding each other with wide eyes of terror. Bastian searched the crowd, scanning every face for a familiar one. He recognized some from 55178, but none of them were Odette.

Dacens waved, motioning for them to follow.

They hesitated, clearly unsure what to do in this new and strange place.

And then the gunfire began again.

053:

Bastian yanked Callum to the ground.

"Odette!" Bastian screamed.

The wind whistled above his head. Bullets thudded into the clones, into the people who'd left their comfortable lives somewhere in a cement city in the sky, only to enter this new world to die. Their bodies smacked the concrete sidewalks, blood pooling into the street.

The crowd erupted into terrified screams. Civilians fled in every direction. Parents shielded their crying children while lone men and women dove for cover. Still, the bullets came, mowing down any unfortunate souls who crossed their paths. Bastian struggled to get to his feet, but Callum or Dacens or someone held him down. He needed to get into the Exportation building. He needed to find Odette.

A bullet ripped through the top of his ear, but he barely noticed it. His heart was pounding so loudly in his chest, his blood was roaring in his ears, and every emotion in his body told him he needed to find Odette.

Somebody pulled Bastian's head. He began to struggle but realized it was only Dacens. The man's dark skin was glistening with sweat, and his sleeve was soaked in blood. "You're okay!" he shouted over the constant gunfire. "You were nicked, but you're fine!" He flicked his ear, indicating where Bastian had been shot.

"Listen!" Dacens shouted. "There's an Elevator just there!" He pointed to a courtyard only a hundred feet away. A monument stood in its center, covered in chalk drawings and clay sculptures. "It'll open any moment and take you down to Earth!" They were crammed in a mass of crouching bodies. People shouted and moved, desperate to find safety.

"You're not coming?" Bastian asked. A body dropped next to them, and he held back a scream.

"I'll come on the next one," Dacens said. He reached into his waistband and pulled out a small gun with a belt of bullets hanging from the bottom. "Get some of these people to the surface, Bastian."

Dacens jumped to his feet and began firing his gun. Bullet casings rained down on Bastian, and he swiped them away before they burned his skin.

A row of people dressed in blue uniforms marched toward the Exportation building. They held long guns to their shoulders and fired straight ahead. Hub City was a bloodbath, and one side was winning.

Bastian watched as Dacens shot down three of the blue uniforms, then ducked back into the crowd.

He'll be fine, Bastian told himself. *Find Odette. Dacens will be fine.*

"Bastian!"

It was Callum. He crawled forward over a couple of dead bodies. His hands were shaking, and his tears had left lines in the dirt on his face. "Bastian, if we don't make it—"

"See that courtyard?" Bastian asked, pointing to the same place Dacens had shown him. "That's an Elevator there. Get as many people there as you can."

"But Bastian—"

"No! We're gonna get out of this. Just trust me."

Before Callum could say another word, Bastian crawled away into the crowd.

Amidst the sweat and the shouting and the gunfire and the blood, Bastian searched every face he could see. He looked for those freckles, those crystal-blue eyes, that long auburn hair tied back by fabric from clothing. He thanked the universe every time he confirmed a corpse wasn't Odette. With every passing moment, every murdered person, he felt the air tighten around him. Each second meant there was less chance he would find her alive.

And then the bullets stopped.

Bastian froze, as did everyone else. It was like the moonlight had stopped time. One second, there was nothing but pure mayhem, and the next, it was as silent as a sleeping child's room.

"STOP!"

Bastian recognized the voice. It boomed through Hub City, bouncing off buildings and echoing down alleys. He didn't even need to see the Boss to know it was him speaking.

Someone grabbed Bastian's hand. He flinched, expecting to see Maeve or Callum, but instead, it was Odette.

Relief exploded through his body. It was a warm wave of overpowering emotions. Before he knew what he was doing, he wrapped Odette in a hug. Most people in the crowd were still crouched or resting on their hands and knees. But Bastian and Odette were now flat on the ground, embraced in a hug so tight that Bastian thought he heard two of his ribs crack.

"Odette," he said, fighting back tears. He pulled away just enough to see her face. Though it'd only been a couple days, he felt like he hadn't seen her in a thousand years, and she looked just as he remembered. Perfect.

"Bastian," she whispered. Her mouth was so close to his. "What's going on?"

The Boss spoke again. His face seemed even more contorted, more demented by the scar on his temple. Standing above the crowd, he was like an immovable giant, one whose very footsteps could kill.

"I demand the leaders of this . . . *rebellion*," he spat the word as if it tasted disgusting in his mouth, "come forward at once."

Nobody moved a muscle. Even Bastian, who so desperately wanted to get Odette to safety, didn't dare breathe.

"Come forward at once," the Boss demanded, his hulking frame covering the distant moon, "or *everyone* dies."

"Bastian," Odette whispered. She pointed to the courtyard. Callum stood between the Elevator doors, holding them open, waving at Bastian and Odette. It was packed with bodies, and even more were clumped around the outside of it, waiting for the next trip down.

"Fine," the Boss said. He raised his hand.

Bastian looked down at Odette. He had a million things left to say to her, and he couldn't decide on even one. He wanted to hold her longer, to kiss her, to show her how he truly felt about her, but there was no time. In a matter of seconds, they would both be filled with bullets.

Maybe there was something beyond death. Maybe they could be reunited there.

She met him with desperate eyes, with a look that said "kiss me" and "hold me" and "I wish there were more time."

She tilted her head just slightly, and the moonlight glinted off her neck.

For the second time in a couple minutes, everything seemed to freeze. The scar on her neck seemed so much bigger, so much more significant than ever before. He'd only noticed it for the first time days earlier. How odd. How unexplainable. If it weren't for his injury, he wouldn't have known about her scar. And if he hadn't known about her scar, there would be no way out of the certain death they were facing.

Bastian stood. He brought Odette with him.

"You," the Boss said, sneering. He grabbed a gun from one of the blue uniforms next to him, strode forward, and when he was five feet away from Bastian, he raised it so it was level with Bastian's eyes. "I don't even know who you are."

"I know," Bastian said. He pulled Odette forward, stepped behind her, and grabbed her neck. She was clearly confused, even scared, but she didn't flinch or move away.

Bastian twisted her head, so her neck was revealed. Though the scar had mostly faded, it was impossible to miss under the harsh lighting of the moon.

The Boss looked at the scar and, for a moment, didn't seem to process what he was staring at.

"I know you lost a daughter years ago," Bastian said. His voice was the only sound in Hub City. It was like the entire world was listening to him. "Someone sent her to one of the towns. You've been looking for her ever since."

Bastian paused. "I know she had a scar on her neck.

I saw you inspect that woman in your office yesterday. You thought she would have a scar just like this, didn't you?" he asked.

The Boss stepped forward. Odette shivered, but she stood firm, gripping Bastian's free hand.

"Yes," the Boss said, his voice now a hoarse whisper. "Just like that." He lifted a finger and stroked the scar on Odette's neck. All at once, his entire face seemed to dismantle. The sneer was replaced with a deep frown. His slanted eyes turned into round orbs. The scar on his temple became nothing more than a wrinkle. In less than a second, the Boss was reduced from the all-powerful figure of a murderous industry to a father who had lost his child.

"My sweet girl," the Boss said.

The gunshot was so loud, it seemed to shatter the sky.

Bastian shut his eyes. The bullet must have hit him. The gunshot had been so close. Only feet away from him. There was no way that it missed his body.

But the pain never came. In a panic, he opened his eyes, immediately scanning Odette for any injuries. Luckily, she seemed to be fine.

In front of them, the Boss twitched. Where once the scar had been on his temple, there was now a gaping hole. Blood trailed from it, trickling into his beard. He fell to his knees, his hands outstretched, his mouth hanging open in shock.

"My sweet girl," he said, the words choked and wet.

He gave one last look to Odette, and then he fell forward on his face.

Behind him, Dacens stood with a gun in his hand, smoke curling away from its barrel.

"Time to go home," he said.

EPILOGUE:

Whenever he slept, Bastian dreamed about the first time he saw the Earth.

After Dacens killed the Boss, the blue uniforms laid down their guns and walked away. Apparently, with no one giving orders, nobody was willing to risk their lives. And on top of all of it, Odette wasn't a clone.

Callum took the first Elevator down along with over a hundred other individuals. Bastian and Odette took the second. Though it'd only been a twenty-minute trip to the Earth's surface, it'd felt like a lifetime. Bastian didn't let go of Odette once the whole trip down.

He hadn't properly prepared himself for the moment the doors opened. The Elevator had come to a clunky, creaking stop. Moments later, the doors had slid open and revealed nothing but green.

Trees, grass, bushes, and vines. They covered the earth. The air was fresh and free of the stale scent of concrete. The ground was soft, and the dirt was cool. The world was filled with sounds of rushing water and all types of bugs chirping.

For the first few hours, as the Elevator brought more and more people to the Earth's surface, Bastian, Odette, and everyone else had merely wandered—looking, touching, smelling, *experiencing* the Earth.

Barely anyone had said a word.

Every night, Bastian dreamt of it, of the first time humanity returned to the Earth's surface. And every time, he woke up smiling.

✳✳✳

Two weeks after they'd arrived on the Earth's surface, Bastian decided it was time.

He woke up in the spot he'd claimed as his own. It was a small patch of grass beneath a giant tree. Many supply trips provided everyone with more of a semblance of life. He'd set up a cot, which was made comfier by many blankets and pillows, and he'd even pitched a sheet of fabric over it all to stop the sap from dripping on him as he slept.

Since the day they'd arrived, people had started building shelters. The elderly were being housed first, and then it would be the women. Bastian knew he'd be one of the last people to get a hut of his own, but he was grateful for that. He loved sleeping under the stars.

"If you don't do it," Callum said, appearing out of nowhere and startling Bastian so bad, he fell out of his cot, "I'm gonna do it for you."

"I don't think anybody would like that," Bastian said, getting to his feet and brushing the dirt from his arms.

"Well, don't say I didn't warn you."

Callum's once skinny frame was now beginning to bulge out. Ever since their third day on the surface, everyone had eaten well. They'd eaten so well, in fact, that many people had thrown up because of overindulgence in food for the first time in their lives. There were plenty of fruits and vegetables in the surrounding area to feed the colony for years. Not only that, but the land was overflowing with animals. Once people had returned to Hub City to bring back weapons, they'd been able to hunt the animals and cook them for food.

"What a life," Callum said.

They still stood beneath Bastian's favorite tree. A few children ran past, giggling and shouting. In the distance, men and women chopped wood and assembled it into structures that would eventually become homes.

"I never told you, Callum." Bastian considered the words he was about to say. He'd had plenty of time to think about them since the night they'd escaped Hub City, and he felt he'd found the right ones.

Bastian continued. "I know that we're clones, that we don't really have any parents or siblings. And while that's a whole psychological issue that's probably gonna haunt us the rest of our lives, I want you to know that you're better than any brother I could have ever asked for."

Callum nodded and clenched his teeth. Birds cawed, and a cloud passed over the sun. The Earth was so green, so gorgeous, so *real*. Not an ounce of concrete in sight. Bastian couldn't believe people had ever willingly left it, even if they had been faced with imminent destruction.

"I'd say something sarcastic right now," Callum responded, "but I won't."

Bastian nodded. Those were probably the most endearing words he would ever hear Callum say, and he was perfectly okay with that.

As Bastian strolled through the land they'd made their home—and what many people were referring to as

"Bliss"—he passed Maeve and Dacens. They were mixing food in a giant wooden bowl.

"You finally gonna do it?" Dacens asked. He was dressed in a tank top and shorts, a far less intimidating look than his last one.

"You better do it," Maeve said, smiling at him. "Or else I'll make you do it."

"Why is everyone so invested in this?" Bastian asked, but even he couldn't hide the smile from his face.

"Because you helped take down the world," Dacens said. "You should be able to do this one small thing."

Bastian rolled his eyes and laughed. He felt good, truly good. He felt like nothing could ruin his good mood.

✱✱✱

He took Odette to the top of a waterfall. He and Callum had found it a few days prior while foraging for food. It was small and quiet, but it was beautiful. The water spilled in broken, splashing streams off a sudden ledge in the landscape, crashing into a shallow lake below. It was surrounded by thick trees, slick rocks, and snaking vines. And as far as Bastian could tell, nobody else had discovered it.

"Why did you bring me here, Bastian?" Odette asked. She wore a slim piece of fabric that hung loosely from her shoulders and stopped just above her knees. Her white skin was sunburned a slight pink, and more freckles had appeared across the bridge of her nose. "I'm not upset," she said, as if she were being interrogated. "About what happened with the Boss. We're not even sure I was his daughter. But even if I was, I'm not upset."

"I know," Bastian said. "That's not why I brought you here."

"Then why did you?"

He took a step closer to her. They stood next to the water, a few feet from where it dropped. Water lapped quietly over their bare feet. Even in the midst of Earth's beauty, Bastian couldn't take his eyes off her.

"Thank you for healing me," Bastian said, motioning to his hands. The bandages were gone now, and the scabs had fallen off. All that was left were faint scars, ones that resembled the scar on her neck. "And for finding me in Hub City. You're always looking out for me. Thank you."

She smiled.

He was glad she didn't have her stethoscope anymore, so she couldn't hear how fast his heart was racing.

"Odette," he said, taking another step closer to her. His hands were on her waist now. He'd waited so long for this. He felt like he couldn't breathe.

He wrapped his hand around the back of her neck, pulled her in, and kissed her.

The nervous tension erupted in his stomach, but he ignored it and pulled her in even closer. Now they were pressed up against each other, wrapped in one another's arms. Her lips were soft. Every time he moved his mouth, or she moved hers, his stomach did another flip. He never wanted the moment to end.

Eventually, though, it did. And instead of returning to Bliss, they sat at the top of the waterfall for quite some time, holding hands, holding each other, dreaming of the future that awaited them.

GAME OVER

As a kid, Tyler H. Jolley always had a knack for storytelling. When he grew bored of old fables, he created his own exciting and unique worlds. Many years later, he still had so many new ideas and stories swirling in his head, but with nowhere to share it. That's when he put his pencil to paper and let the creative juices flow.

His debut novel, *Extracted*, came out in 2013 and swiftly became an Amazon Best Seller and Spencer Hill Press Best Seller. *Prodigal and Riven*, the second and third books in The Lost Imperials series were released in May of 2015.

After a brief hiatus he restructured and returned to writing. His Adventurous Ali series has received much praise. To date, he's released four in the series.

When he's not writing, you can find him at his orthodontic practice, mountain biking, or on the hunt for the perfect doughnut.

www.ingramcontent.com/pod-product-compliance
Lightning Source LLC
Chambersburg PA
CBHW021319190726
48288CB00003B/885